Beneath The Mimosa Tree
—A Novel—

♥

Stephanie Verni

Beneath the Mimosa Tree is a work of fiction. Names, characters, and places are the product of the author's imagination. Actual places in the novel are used fictitiously. Resemblances to actual persons, living or dead, events, locales, or establishments is coincidental.

Cover image & author photograph by Jennifer Bumgarner.

Beneath the Mimosa Tree

ISBN-13: 978-0615617749
ISBN-10: 0615617743

For those who have made mistakes in the past,
for those who have tried to correct them,
and for my family with love.

♥

Part One

Annabelle

I left Cole four weeks ago. The cool and crisp weather, combined with the autumn breeze, filled the air with the fresh scent of leaves. Despite the end of what was a tumultuous relationship, I felt a sense of renewal. I hardly recognized myself when I caught a glimpse of my reflection in the mirror. It seemed as if someone else was staring back at me.

It was a Saturday morning, and I was enjoying its laziness after surviving a hectic week at work. I had a batch of chocolate chip pumpkin cookies baking in the oven. I planned on taking them to an Oktoberfest party I'd been invited to later in the evening. There were still moving boxes scattered all over my condo, but I was able to find some of the necessary baking supplies—a spatula, mixing bowl, and baking sheet. I figured a heaping plate of cookies and a twelve-pack of dark beer would be appropriate to bring to the party my friend Will and his girlfriend, Linda, were hosting.

There was something therapeutic about time alone in the morning. There was no makeup to apply, the bed could be left unkempt if I chose not to make it, and I was actually able to read every section of the newspaper, including the sports section, without having to share it or refold the paper back to its original state. I tightened the belt of my pink cotton bathrobe and stepped out onto my patio with a cup of coffee. If I strained my neck to the left just far enough, I could see Spa Creek. I couldn't afford the condo with full water view, so this one would do. Plus, it was all mine. As a thirty-two year old woman, I decided it was time I actually owned property. Cole and I had been renting an apartment in Baltimore, but toward the end of the summer when I knew the relationship was over, I did some digging—a former colleague of mine owned it and had moved on to a position with a university in Pennsylvania. It hadn't sold, and after looking at it, I knew it would be perfect for me. It had been on the market since May, so I picked up the phone and called him about possibly purchasing it. He was thrilled to hear of my excitement for the place. I was more than ready to leave a bigger city in favor of the smaller one where I worked. Annapolis was my home, and although it could bring back melancholy feelings at times, it was the one place where I felt entirely comfortable. I closed on the property last week, and the movers set me up two days ago. It was amazing what you could accomplish when you put your mind to it.

I worked at the small college in town as a professor, and on days when it wasn't too cold or too hot, I would stroll to work. Walking was a welcome change from the forty-five minute commute I'd endured for the last three years. It was always Cole's proximity to work that was most important; it was always Cole's wants and interests that took precedence over mine. I don't know why I stayed with him for as long as I did, except maybe that it was some form of self-inflicted punishment.

It no longer mattered; I was free. I'd left that world behind, and it wasn't the first time I'd ever done something like that. Years ago, I made a similar decision, though it was hardly fair to compare the two. The last time I left, I was full of regret and sorrow. In this particular case, I only regretted wasting so much time.

* * *

I walked up Main Street and couldn't help but become en-amored with the crisp, blue sky and white fluffy clouds as they hung over the city and made it look postcard perfect. The wooden dome of the Capital building graced the city, and the streets had come alive with shoppers walking and window shopping, pushing baby strollers loaded with bags, and watching the fudge makers in the storefront window. I loved being back. I sat among the other people who were doing as I was doing—people watching. This spot was a good one, right at the tip of the dock overlooking the harbor and all its visitors.

I contemplated this change I'd made in my life. I knew I would have much more time alone, something I'd never been completely comfortable with or ever fully embraced. I wondered how long my positive outlook would last. As much as Cole was absolutely not the right man for me, and my decision to dissolve that relation-ship was the right one, there was something unsettling about being single again. Attending Will's party alone was somewhat liberat-ing, though I knew it would take some adjustment. I didn't want to answer any questions about Cole or our breakup. I was through talking about it.

In fact, last night, when I curled up in bed and adjusted to my new surroundings, I listened to the quiet ticking of my English clock. Being alone was peaceful. I was free from confrontation, mistrust, and insults. I didn't miss him. Not once.

* * *

I arrived much later to Will's house than I had intended. While all of our mutual friends couldn't make the party, some would be there, and I was anxious about having to make small talk and answer questions about my personal life.

As I approached the back gate, I saw the party was in full swing, and I offered my cookies and beer to Linda as she was greeting her guests there. It was Will's house—walking distance from my own—and though Linda didn't formally share his address, she stayed there most of the time. Will was a writer for the city's newspaper as well as a freelancer for a handful of national magazines. We met several years ago when I was in search of a guest speaker for my classroom. I called the newspaper, asked him to come, and our friendship blossomed after that.

"Annabelle," Will shouted as he waved from across the lawn. He had a tent set up in the backyard and little lanterns lighting the walkways throughout. He lived in Murray Hill, one of the historic areas in the city of Annapolis, and his place was the perfect size for a small gathering. Bavarian music played, and beer cans and bottles formed a pyramid on the open table.

"Hi, Will," I said, as I leaned in to give him a peck on the cheek. "Nice set up."

"We try. I'm so glad you made it. You look fantastic. How's the new place?"

"Good, thanks. I'm getting used to it. When do you want to come by? I can make you a gourmet dinner."

"Oh, I don't know, soon. I think Linda's a little uneasy about our friendship now that you and Cole are kaput."

"You're kidding," I said. "She was fine when I got here."

"Maybe. But she's watching us like a hawk now. Can I get you a beer?"

"I'd love one."

He walked away from me and I turned slightly to see if I could catch a glimpse of Linda and her newfound paranoia. She was nowhere in sight, but just knowing she was suspicious made me uncomfortable. Will and I were close—I considered him one of my dearest friends—and up to about five minutes ago had been happy with his choice of Linda as a girlfriend and potential wife. She'd never exhibited any signs of jealousy where I was concerned, though there was that one colleague of Will's I remembered her groaning about one night at dinner. So, maybe it wasn't just me who troubled her.

I stood by myself for a while and felt burdened by the lack of a companion. I knew I should have moved from the spot I'd attached myself to and mingled, but I was also dreading the questions of where Cole was from folks who knew me. He had attended parties here before. He could put on a show; he was a stellar joke teller, and could hold court with stories that seemed to entertain both the men and the ladies.

At the picnic table, a group of Will's friends were playing "I Never," a somewhat immature game that involved telling the truth about things you'd never done before, though I was pretty sure there was a lot of lying going on throughout it. My head started to become light, and I dismissed myself from the table and searched for something to eat. At that point, my stomach rumbled because I hadn't eaten anything substantial since I grabbed a frozen yogurt from the City Dock Café earlier.

I made a plate of food—German sausage, potato salad, and some sauerkraut—and turned to find a place to sit. I dove right in.

"Annabelle? Annabelle Marco?"

"Yes," I mumbled through an overzealous bite of the sausage.

"Jeez, I haven't seen you in years!"

"Andrew, oh my gosh! Wow! So good to see you."

For a moment I thought the sausage was going to become

lodged in my throat. I reached for my beer and swallowed hard trying to get it down. Seeing my discomfort, he quickly handed me a napkin.

"Yes," he said. "It's been a long time."

He appeared different than the last time I saw him. His hair was receding, and he looked as if he'd lost weight. He was still wearing his wire-rimmed glasses, but it was his nice smile and straight teeth I remembered most. He shook my hand. Soft palms.

"So where do you live?" I asked.

"Here, in Annapolis. I'm a pediatrician. My office is near Parole Plaza. And you?"

"I teach English at the college."

He smiled at me, shaking his head. "It's such a coincidence."

"Really?"

"Yes, well, you know Michael and I spent several years together in London, though he stayed there when I came home. But I just spoke with him a few days ago and apparently he's decided to move back to the area. Did you know?"

"No. No, I didn't."

I tried to hide both my surprise and panic, though I knew I was probably not succeeding, and I suddenly wished I were a better actress. I realized I couldn't hold on much longer, so I needed to either change the subject or walk away. I tried the former.

"So, how do you know Will?"

"I'm engaged to Sarah, Linda's friend."

"Oh, well, congratulations. That's nice. I don't believe I've met her."

"Yes, thank you. She's great. Oh, as a matter of fact, she's waving to me over there. I'm supposed to be her partner in a game of pool. Guess I'd better get to it. It was nice seeing you, Annabelle," he said.

"You, too, Andrew." I couldn't bring myself to utter *give my best to Michael*. Instead, I just smiled and waved as he walked away.

I threw the rest of my plate into the garbage, having barely touched the potato salad and sauerkraut, as my appetite morphed into nausea. Andrew and his mention of Michael ruined what had been a perfectly good day. Confronting this news at Will's party—a place where I was supposed to be safe, learning how to be single and trying to have a good time in a sea of couples—was too much for me. I wanted to move my legs and walk. I felt claustrophobic. At least Linda would be happy I was leaving.

* * *

My head felt heavier than it did when I was playing "I Never" with Will's friends. I felt overwhelmed, uneasy. I walked down Duke of Gloucester Street and cut over to the City Dock. There were boats moving in and out on the glass-like water, and the streets were busy with a steady Saturday night crowd. The bars that surrounded the harbor were packed, and music blared from a couple of anchored boats; happy sounds of people sharing good times filled the night air. The moon was high, its shine glistening off the still water where I sat and dangled my feet above the gentle waves of the harbor's waters.

My parents were scheduled to return from Florida tomorrow, and I was supposed to play taxi and pick them up at the airport. It felt like an eternity until they would arrive. I'd planned to ask them what they knew of Michael's impending return to Annapolis—or did Andrew just say "the area?" Did that mean Maryland, East Coast, or the States? I couldn't remember; the conversation seemed like it had taken place years ago, as opposed to minutes ago amidst the sound of accordions and guitars that set the party scene at Will's house. When Andrew mentioned it had been ten years, the reality of the passage of time sunk in. I saw myself as a completely different person. I'd grown up, become more independent, even if I did stay with Cole for too long. I should have left him when my mother was ill, but I was too distraught. The thought of how Cole behaved during that time sent chills up my spine, and not in a good way. But Michael—Michael could seep through my pores and jump start my heart from across an ocean. I wondered when he'd come home. Or had he already arrived? I knew someday I'd come face-to-face with this reality.

I reminded myself that what I'd heard was only hearsay, and nothing would be confirmed until I talked with my parents. Did they know? Had the Contellis shared this information with my parents and my parents not shared it with me?

The blaring of a boat horn caught me off guard and startled me. I checked my watch. It was almost midnight. I got up, brushed myself off, and began the walk home, examining each man I passed on the street, studying his build, looking at his face, and wondering.

* * *

My parents' flight was on time, which was a miracle considering the hurricane warnings that had been issued for the Florida panhandle. My parents were lucky; they were able to take their regularly scheduled flight and made it home safely without incident.

My mother looked well, which lightened my heart. Her battle

with breast cancer over the past two years had not been an easy one. When they found it, she was diagnosed stage two, but with surgery and chemotherapy, she became a survivor. Sometimes I worried that her petite, frail body would not sustain the endless hours of post-chemo vomiting. Her constant sunny disposition helped get her through. Her hair did grow back, though she kept it very short, but her pretty face could pull it off. Plus, as she said, "It's only hair," which put life into perspective. She was required to be checked and scanned every few months, and I knew the fear of the cancer returning consumed her. However, all reports indicated the cancer was gone, and we were all thankful for that.

"You look great," I said to her as I took her bags and put them in the trunk of my car. "Nicely bronzed and relaxed."

"I feel great. That was the best three weeks. The only thing that would have made it better would have been if you had joined us. But I know you've been busy. How's the new place? I can't wait to see it."

"It's good, Mom. It looks a little different than when you last saw it. The painters were in two days before the movers unloaded my stuff, so it's got some color and it looks nice with my things. I could use a few more pieces, though. I figured you might want to go shop for some with me."

"I'd love to, sweetheart," she said.

"How's the campus?" My mother was always infinitely proud of my occupation.

"Great," I said. "Classes are going well so far."

My dad kissed me on the cheek and put his luggage in the car. We buckled up and began our ride home.

"So, no word from Cole?" my father asked.

"No, why? Were you expecting him to ride up on his white

horse and try to win me back?

"Funny, Annabelle."

My parents never liked Cole, mostly because he couldn't hold a job and his tendency to drink too much turned my father off. My father never tolerated immature men, and since he regularly called Cole "juvenile," he probably jumped for joy when I left him. It was remarkable how your parents never stopped being your parents, no matter how old you were. Even when they attempted to bite their tongues, I always had a strong understanding of where they stood on major decisions and issues. And though my father never said as much, I think the fact that Cole was not who he'd pick for me as a partner had a great deal to do with both his initial and continued dislike of him. My father spoke Italian, both his parents were from Italy, and I believed he always had it in his head that I'd settle down with a nice Italian boy. Michael was always his particular choice.

"I ran into an old friend of Michael Contelli's last night at a party and found out that he's moving back to the area. Did you two know this?" I blurted out the words.

There was an eerie silence. Apparently, no one wanted to answer the question. I waited for one of them to respond as I listened to the hum of the car.

My mother fielded the question. "Well, yes, we did hear about it from Carol and Remzi." Another moment of silence passed. I mulled over what I would say next.

"Were you trying to keep it from me?" I asked in an accusatory tone.

"Not exactly. It's just, well, we never really know how to broach the subject of Michael with you. We never know where it will go."

"Go? It hasn't gone anywhere in ten years, Mom. Where the

heck do you think it will go now?"

My father cleared his throat. He was worried I'd get emotional and become distracted behind the wheel. "I think what your mother is saying is, we didn't know how to tell you or how you might handle it. I'm hoping you're going to handle it well, especially while you're driving."

"I'm fine, Dad. I just wish I'd heard it from you both. It caught me off-guard last night, and the whole thing has never been sorted out, so that makes me uncomfortable. Is he moving back to the States or back to Annapolis or what?"

"From what his mother tells me, he's coming back to Annapolis for a bit, but he may have a job opportunity in New York. We don't know yet. We think he's going to live with Carol and Remzi for a little while."

A rush of adrenaline coursed through my body as my emotions became a conglomeration of anger, hostility, and anxiety. I knew eventually the inevitable would happen; I couldn't hide forever like I tried to do in the past. If he were going to live with his parents for a stretch of time, I knew our paths would cross. It would undoubtedly happen because my parents and his parents still lived next door to each other in Pendennis Mount across the Severn River Bridge. Both of their properties overlooked the water and the Naval Academy, though our house was perched a little higher than theirs. Meticulous landscaping and a row of very large arborvitae trees also protected their home. However, the fact remained that they'd been neighbors for twenty-seven years. And best friends for twenty.

* * *

Spending time alone in my condo afforded me vast amounts of time to think. In fact, having too much time to think caused me to reflect on things I'd done—and not done—in my life. I wondered why I'd made the mistakes I'd made in the past or how I could have forsaken someone I loved wholeheartedly. Then, I endured the even more painful memories of allowing myself to move forward years later as I wondered why someone else treated me with disdain and why I tolerated it for so long. I rationalized my own expectations with regard to my personal relationships. I questioned how I could have done the things I did—after all, I was intelligent and had a solid, respectable job. I came from a loving (if somewhat controlling) family; I contributed to charities, even on a small salary; I tried to attend mass regularly; and I did reasonably well at staying in shape and caring for myself. And yet, I would take these moments to evaluate and scrutinize the colossal mistakes I had made along the way. I began to wonder if spending that much time alone was therapeutic or damaging.

My paralyzing thoughts were broken when the phone rang. It was eight o'clock. I'd already graded one stack of papers.

"Hello."

"Hi. You alone?"

"Yes, why? Who did you think would be here?"

"I guess I thought maybe Cole?"

"Will! For crying out loud, there's no more Cole."

"Well, you've said that once or twice before."

"Yeah? Well, this time I mean it. Great party last night. How's my friend Linda?"

"Fine. She's at her place. Want to meet at Fran O'Brien's for dinner?"

I looked around my condo at the mess that had become less

messy with each box I'd broken down and stacked in the corner of the dining room. I convinced myself that I needed to stay home and wallow in my own misery. I knew I needed to unpack more boxes, sort things out, and get organized. I took a deep breath.

"How soon can you meet me there?" I asked.

* * *

We ordered a bottle of Chardonnay and two crab cake platters while we sat at the bar overlooking Main Street. It wasn't surprising that there was a sparse crowd. Fran's was a landmark city restaurant. It featured dark woods, ambient lighting, and a dance floor upstairs, though no thumping could be heard through the floor that night. Saturday nights were typically the busiest, and the place was known for attracting both the locals and the tourists.

Will held up his glass for a toast. "Here's to your new-found freedom," he said.

"Cheers," I said. We clinked glasses and commented on the dryness of the wine.

"Did you tell Linda you were going out with me tonight?"

"Actually, you'll be proud of me. I did tell her."

"And she's handling it well?"

"Not really. I think she's pretty pissed at me. She can't understand why I'd want to be out with you instead of her."

I looked at him for a second because poor Linda had a point. Why would he be out with me when he could be cavorting with the woman he loved?

"So, what did you say?"

"I told her, 'Listen, Linda. I go out with Annabelle because she's one of my best buds. Just because she and Cole broke up doesn't mean we can't be friends.'"

"Sounds logical—and true. But she didn't go for it?"

"Not really."

"You should've told her to join us," I said.

"Nah. I'm allowed to hang out with you. Just you," he said.

"That's right," I said, teasing him. "Just the buddies."

"You know what I mean."

I liked that he took a stand with Linda. Just because we happened to be of the opposite sex didn't mean we wanted to date each other. Will and I had survived on a pretty solid friendship, and my recent single status shouldn't have warranted concern.

"Truthfully," he continued, "I was worried about you. I know you had your 'happy face' on last night, and it was good of you to come, but you sort of ran out the door and I wasn't sure you were okay."

After I'd talked with Andrew and pitched my food, I did make a quick exit. Will questioned why I was leaving, and I assured him I was fine—that I was just tired. I didn't tell him about Andrew and what he'd told me of Michael; Will didn't know the whole story of Michael because that relationship happened long before I met Will. I wasn't one to share my sordid past, even with my closest of friends. However, in light of the recent developments, and, because the landscape of the story had the potential to change, I knew I'd have to unburden myself to Will. I considered telling him. I considered confessing my secret, but in some way it still felt like a betrayal.

Which was quite ironic. When Michael and I first got together, no one knew about us. We were the only ones. We kept it hidden, locked away from our parents and our friends. It was as it always should have been—just between us.

For a moment I let my mind wander back to a time that was simple and easy. I imagined Michael sitting across from me, throwing his head back in uproarious laughter, smiling with that devilish twinkle in his eye. I wondered how he looked and if he still wore that old, torn army jacket that belonged to his father.

"Annabelle, did you hear me? I asked if you want me to speak to your class this semester. Are you okay?"

The truth was, I didn't really know how I was.

"Actually, I'm not okay," I said to him. "Have I ever mentioned Michael Contelli before?"

In the span of forty-five minutes, I recounted an abridged story of Michael to a man whose own face looked betrayed by this past I'd kept from him.

* * *

Will let me talk and then gave me a lift home. I thanked him for listening to me so attentively and appreciated his time. He didn't judge me and suggested that what happened took place a long time ago. His words should have been comforting, but they weren't.

I crawled into bed and found myself staring at the ceiling, the streetlamps casting a slight glow into my room. Last year, when my mother's condition was at its gravest and she was sweating and shivering from chemotherapy, I hardly slept. I stayed at her house with my father, and the two of us did our best to care for her. My friends knew the toll her illness took on our family and often made meals and stopped over to offer support. For a brief period, I set up camp in their home in my old bedroom. On the weekends, I worked in my mother's Italian pastry shop, so she didn't feel she had to be there or worry about her staff. My mother's store opened its doors when I was ten; after taking summer cuisine courses in France and Italy, and months after returning home, my mother decided to open La Pancia Affamata, Italian for "The Hungry Tummy." Local food writers praised my mother's pastries; she received many write-ups in local newspapers, and she achieved a certain level of notoriety. Her little bakery was a landmark in Annapolis.

When she was sweating profusely one afternoon, and I was applying cold cloths to her forehead, her hair falling out, her spirits shattered, her eyes weary and sad, I sat by her side, holding her hand as she fought through the nausea.

"I'm going to sell that bakery if I get well. I have prospective buyers," she said.

"Mom, you're going to get well. You're going to beat this cancer. You are your bakery; you can't sell it. People go there because of you."

"Do you want it, Annabelle? It's yours if you want it."

I wanted my mother to beat cancer more than anything, and the fact that she was asking me if I wanted the bakery scared me. It made me feel as if she were giving up. Plus, I didn't want to hurt her feelings. I adored that bakery—just the smell of it reminded me of her—but it was not what I wanted to do as an occupation. I already had one I loved.

It was during the worst part of her illness that she told me Michael had divorced. "When?" I asked.

"I'm not sure. I only just heard it from Carol when she came to see me the other day. It had been so long, we had catching up to do, and I just missed that part," she said.

Carol Contelli and my mother had been best friends until tensions rose and it became difficult for them to sift through the aftermath. It was just easier for them to avoid one another altogether as the blame always fell on me, and then, by default, our family.

When my mother finally fell asleep that day, I found my father organizing his power tools in the shed behind the house.

"What are you up to?" I asked.

"Busy work," he said. "I have to find things to occupy my time or I can get so…" His voice started to crack. I put my arm around him.

"I know, Dad. But you can't show her you're worried. Do you know she's talking about selling the bakery? I hope she's not giving up, because it's not over."

I told my father to come and sit with me on the veranda, a word for our deck that made us all laugh. It had rained earlier, but had tapered off and the skies were clearing. My father said he was certain there would be a pink sky tonight. Some people enjoyed a picturesque blue sky, others enjoyed big fluffy clouds, but my father and I were pink sky enthusiasts. Near sundown, Maryland pink skies were to be admired. The veranda was our hangout. From it, the river was in full view looking west; sailboats drifted by as they made their way into Annapolis, the bridge in the distance shuffled traffic to and from Ocean City, and visible osprey nests sat high atop the boat markers. My father was an architect and loved to use architectural words, so he insisted, from the day it was completed, that we call it a veranda; because it was a vast structure on the back of the house, he said that he worked too hard and saved too long for it to simply be called a deck. And so the choice word was selected, though my mother could hardly say it with a straight face, and when she did, she usually drew it out like a 1940s movie star: "Ver-an-duh."

"See? See what I told you?" my father said that night after dinner as we helped my mother outside, gently placing her frail, petite body on the cushioned two-seat glider, knowing she needed some fresh air on the veranda. "I knew that there would be a pink sky. Damn if I wasn't right. I wanted you to see this, and not from the window."

"Pink skies are definitely best from the ver-an-duh," my mother said, her tired voice more shaky than usual, but giving us her very best Bette Davis imitation. I saw her squeeze my dad's hand, her head propped up against his shoulder, his arm around her, as they gently rocked back and forth. I also saw my dad surreptitiously dab a tear from the corner of his eye.

None of us slept much during those days, as anxiety and worry consumed us. I started seeing my therapist, Delia, at that time, though I'd never told anyone I sought counseling; she helped me cope with things that I had no control over. The possible death of my mother was too much for me to bear, and I didn't feel I could talk to my father about it—I didn't want to burden him with my own fears.

I hadn't felt anxiety like that until I learned that Michael was coming back. At times I let myself remember our relationship fondly, but for the most part I tried as hard as I could to forget. Unfortunately, that tactic had never been entirely effective.

I considered getting out of bed and turning on the television. I knew it was going to be a restless night. I never had the good fortune of being a good sleeper. In fact, the inability to sleep was one of the worst afflictions in the world. It was utterly frustrating and debilitating. One sleepless night was acceptable. Two sleepless nights were less desirable, but conquerable. Add a third, fourth, fifth, and sixth one in for good measure, and a catastrophic mess unfolded. Being irritable during the day or having the overwhelming need to crawl under your desk for a siesta was not going to get you places in this world. I had a job where mood swings were not welcomed or professional. No one wanted a teacher who yawned through lectures or student presentations. Sleep should have been a priority for me, but during that time of my life, it wasn't the case.

I was probably also expecting to have the dream again. I'd been the victim of a recurring dream that haunted me and made me feel abnormal. I'd been having it for years, but when I was unusually stressed, the dream was vivid and realistic; I would wake up clenching something or drenched in sweat. In my restless state, I was unable to think of anyone but Michael. Just like that, he was able to take over and occupy my thoughts. My relationship with Cole was less than stellar, as were the few I had before I became involved with him. Not surprisingly, my own relationship with my family weathered battles of its own, though it had become better over time. Vivi, my grandmother, was instrumental in keeping me grounded and was always my biggest supporter; she helped me get through Michael, my parents, and my mother's illness. I always relied on her and looked to her often for guidance.

My expectations of love certainly dwindled. It didn't matter how I tried to uncork repressed feelings or whether I allowed myself to stay in an unsatisfactory and unfulfilling relationship. None of it mattered. The fact was, when I thought of Michael, what I was left with was an abiding sense of sadness and remorse, my own little purgatory.

Michael

It was late. I was restless again. Bloody hell. I'd shaken my hangover about four hours ago, and I was sick of being in my tiny, claustrophobic, empty flat, so I decided to take a walk through Covent Garden. It was a Sunday night, but the city didn't sleep. In fact, Covent Garden was never quiet. Time of day made no difference in that place. And even though it was often crawling with tourists, there were plenty of Londoners who had an affinity for the place as well. I always loved London, its vibrant people, its rich and noble history, so different than that of America. And yet, I was ready to go back to the States. I had absolutely no idea where I'd end up permanently. I just knew it was time to go home.

I'd been in London just over ten years. I'd spent four of them attending graduate school part-time at the University of London. There were many people I'd miss, from professors I'd become close with to other students and work colleagues, and my two best mates, Janie and her husband Billy. I pictured the two of them completely knackered; they threw the best goodbye party ever last night, and it happened to have been in my honor. Their flat in Notting Hill had been jammed with about eighty rowdy people. Wall to wall blokes and ladies. My ears were ringing from the blaring music. Every time I saw Janie, she had a drink in each hand, and Billy was holding court in the kitchen playing rounds and rounds of Fuzzy Duck; it was such a raucous party we could hardly hear each other's responses during the game, which made it even funnier.

I'd been at *The Times* for six years, and Janie was my partner in crime. She and I were assistant editors, and had she not been there, I would have missed out on the friendship I had with her and Billy, in addition to getting to know to the multitude of wacky friends they shared. The two of them were the most social people I knew. As much as they wanted children, it wasn't in the cards for them, and so their outlet was to have a good time—all the time. Their front door was a revolving door. I could probably count on my fingers the number of times they hadn't hosted weekend guests since I'd known them.

"Mikey, you want to come over and have a nosh up?" Janie asked me three weeks ago, the day after I had made my decision to leave, unbeknownst to her.

"Sure. Sounds good."

"I'm making up my mother's roast. First time I've attempted the recipe, so don't raise your hopes too high."

"Your cooking has never been—"

She cut me off. "The bee's knees?" She winked.

"I didn't say that," I said.

"You didn't have to. But it doesn't matter. We'll have a pint and it will make it all better."

Earlier in the day, I had submitted my resignation to my boss, a man named Albert, who had wrinkles on his face deeper than the Grand Canyon and a booming, deep voice. He was a gruff old bloke, and was easily one of the tallest people I'd ever come in contact with; I often had to strain my neck to meet his eyes. I ended up liking him more than I expected. He was a brilliant editor, and his attention to detail taught me writing skills that would last me a lifetime.

"So, what's back in America for you then, Mike?" he asked me.

"My family. My folks are getting older, and I've been away from them now for ten years. I'm an only child and it's time for me to go home."

I'd thought it over long and hard. I knew if I didn't leave London now I may never have gone.

He patted me on the back, accepted my resignation, and wished me well. Now all I had to do was tell everyone else. And that wasn't going to be easy.

When I arrived at Janie's the house smelled inviting, but I held back my enthusiasm. She was, indeed, a notorious failure in the kitchen. It was a shame because she was enamored with cooking shows, held Julia Child in the highest esteem, and knew every five-star restaurant in the city. Billy loved to try to make sense of and explain her cooking handicap. "She either undercooks it or over-cooks it, it's never spot on," he would say, which explained the pile of takeaway menus in the corner on the counter near the cookie jar. There must have been close to one hundred stacked high.

I wasn't looking forward to telling them that night, not because I thought they wouldn't understand, but because I knew they'd bombard me with questions about why I was leaving. I was hoping Janie wasn't going to try to Freud me with her psychoanalytical bullshit about Lisbeth again, but even two years later, that discussion continued to fascinate her. Lisbeth and I were long over; I'd had other girlfriends, but no one in particular since then. It wasn't tragic. I was actually enjoying my freedom. I started running again, and the gym was a place for me to unwind. I'd never been in better physical shape. The exercise and my own freedom were agreeing with me. I'd even started writing in my spare time again.

When the timer went off, Billy, Janie and I huddled around the oven as if it were ready to give birth. We were eager to see what would emerge.

"I hope it's not still breathing," Billy said.

"Maybe it's cooked down to the size of a hockey puck," I cracked.

"You two! Go away and drink your pints," she said, whacking us with her hot mitt. "Drink up and it won't matter what the hell the food tastes like!"

No one disliked Janie. It was difficult to be mad at her even for a second. Her husband could attest to that better than anyone. "She's a lovely little wicked bird," he'd said of her one night, "sweet and cracking, and everyone's best friend." It didn't hurt that she was an adorable little thing—a spitfire, as she was often called at work. She had dark hair, a smart pointy nose, glowing skin, and a body that showed off the aerobics classes she took every week. Saying so-long to the two of them was going to be the toughest thing about leaving. They always made me feel comfortable in their home, and I'd spent countless hours watching football with them, playing cards, or throwing back a pint or two.

We toasted the roast, and began to dive into it. It wasn't half bad.

"I don't believe it, Janes! It's actually not horrible," I said.

"Should we call the local news? Should Julia Child be notified?" Billy said.

"Go ahead, yuck it up. I knew one day I'd present something delectable."

We passed the potatoes, also done to near perfection, and the rice dish was somewhat pleasing to the palate. I decided to just blurt it out.

"Well, since Janie has finally concocted something actually worth eating, I feel that I can now officially leave you, Billy, in very good hands." They both looked at me. "I've decided to leave."

"You can't leave, Mikey. We just sat down!" Billy said.

"No...no...I mean, I've decided to leave London. I'm moving back to the States."

The two of them were gobsmacked.

"What are you on about?" Billy asked.

"No worries, Billy," Janie said, tapping his arm lightly, "he's just having a laugh."

"Actually, I'm not. I resigned today, and I've already been let out of my flat. I found someone who will take it over, so there were no problems. I leave in three weeks."

They were processing what I had said. I was sure they were wondering why I hadn't told them before. Over the course of ten years, I'd learned that the best decisions were the ones you made by yourself. You didn't need outside influences to help, nor did you need to put stock in anyone else. You avoided disappointment that way.

Janie started to turn on the waterworks. "This is all very abrupt, isn't it? Why? You must tell us why you are leaving."

I put my fork down and leaned my arms on the table. "Honestly, I just feel this need to be home, to see my folks, to reconnect with old friends."

"Does this have anything to do with your ex-fiancee?" Janie asked.

"No. Nothing. The last I heard of her was she was living with someone in Baltimore. This has nothing to do with her, Lisbeth, you two, or anyone. It has to do with me. I'm ready to move on, or move back, or whatever. Trust me, I've really thought it over. I never expected to stay this long in the first place. I thought I was going to move home after grad school, but I ended up staying, and I'm glad I did."

The two of them stopped eating. They stared at me in disbelief.

Billy broke the silence. "Well, you know how we feel. We're going to miss your sorry ass. But no need for tears; we'll have one hell of a cheerio piss-up, right Janie-girl?" he said.

* * *

I left Covent Garden, and headed down to the Charing Cross
Piers. When I first came to London, I studied journalism. I spent
countless hours at the Piers getting story ideas and interviewing
people. There were people who had lived in London all their lives,
those who were visiting for the first time, immigrants and expatri-
ates. I recalled one girl in particular with a bruised eye and red
marks all up and down her arm. She actually spoke to me when I
was writing a story on London and its people. She came to London
from Sweden. "I'm getting away from a horrible boyfriend," she
said. There were stories all around us, and my job was to dig and
find them. I missed the writing, though editing had become my
livelihood.

It seemed as if I had arrived only yesterday, incensed, sad,
depressed, and in disbelief over what had happened to me. I was
no longer that person. Over the course of ten years, my story had
been in London, but it started long before that. Some things were
tougher to shake than others; some things were more difficult to
overcome. I wondered how my own story would unfold over the
next ten years and where my life would take me beyond this great
city of London.

* * *

I reclined the best that I could in my coach class seat bound for
Baltimore Washington International Airport. I despised airports.
Thoroughly loathed them, in fact. I rarely traveled on planes except

for overnight trips to Paris, Rome, or Barcelona. I'd only been home to visit five times in ten years. My folks came to see me; it ended up that we alternated visits. But it was the airport I detested, the smells, the sterility of the place, the anonymous voices on the loudspeaker telling you what to do. I never liked seeing people by themselves, lost, trying to find their way to a gate or to collect their luggage. The whole airport experience left me frustrated and drained.

In Italy, I took the Eurail from Rome to Venice, and it was the most pleasant experience. People were friendlier on trains—they talked, shared sports pages, and instigated gossip sessions. The atmosphere was festive on a train. I'd never found it to be true for air travel. People wanted to sit in their space and stare straight ahead.

I sat in my coach seat, but had the good sense to book one at the window—and kept to myself. I had a book, newspapers, magazines, and a notebook to write any ideas that came to me on the flight. I'd arranged to have the things I couldn't fit into my suitcase shipped home and expected them to arrive within two weeks. My furniture had been shipped to the States, as well. In the meantime, I had enough clothes to get me through several days, and I knew that I might have to buy a suit if I was actually serious about some of the interview prospects I'd been pursuing.

When I opened my notebook, the only card I kept from Lisbeth, the one I found in the envelope when the finalized divorce papers were delivered, fell onto the tray. It was a bit worn on the edges and creased. I opened it and read it for the hundredth time; the economy of her words was still astonishing.

Mike,
I'm sorry it didn't work out between us. I often wonder if you

ever really loved me. Have a good life,
    --Lisbeth

There was no doubt Lisbeth had a flair for the dramatic; she was a part-time actress who performed in local productions and sang with a small band on the weekends in Oxford. She was attractive, with long, sandy brown hair and a beauty mark by her lip. She loved to wear low-cut, short dresses that showed off her cleavage and her legs, her two best assets. When I recalled the pair of us together now, in hindsight, I realized we had absolutely nothing in common. During the two years I was with her, I don't believe she ever picked up a book. She was absolutely useless when it came to current news, which was bloody ironic because it was my livelihood. If it didn't relate to Princess Di's gowns or Gucci's newest handbag, she had a hard time participating in a conversation.

There was something inherently wrong from the start. In the end, I guess I married her because I was lonely. But I knew right away that I couldn't stay in a relationship that wasn't right. We simply didn't fit.

When I realized marrying Lisbeth was a mistake, I wondered if that was how Annabelle felt about me those many years ago. If Annabelle had indeed felt that way about me, she had every right to leave. Every right. I never wanted to admit that.

One afternoon, months after my divorce from Lisbeth, I was having coffee in the break room with Janie. We were discussing my short-lived marriage.

"Do you ever think about Lisbeth?" Janie asked.

"Only once in a blue moon," I said honestly.

"Did you ever love her?"

"Not the way you should love someone if you have a chance at a long-lasting relationship like yours and Billy's."

Janie leaned over and refilled my coffee. "You've never told me, but I would guess that somebody ripped out that heart of yours a while ago and it hasn't quite been put back in the right spot."

I smiled. That was exactly why Janie and I could be terrific friends: her directness and her ability to understand me had all the makings of best friend material. She was right. I never talked to anyone but Andrew about my previous relationship, and then only very little. I probably could have benefitted from it. I was never able to discuss it, but I did give Janie the *Reader's Digest* version.

There were times I thought that if there had been no Billy, I might have allowed myself to fall for Janie—she understood me, got my sense of humor, and we laughed all the time. It made me think about timing. I'd experienced a lot of crap timing all around. Romantic thoughts of Janie would creep into my head, and I'd find myself taking walks during lunch breaks to clear my head or saying no to coffee in the morning at the shop around the corner with her to keep things at bay. I wondered sometimes if she didn't feel something, too, but it was never addressed. I wasn't the type to destroy a happy home and what seemed to be a near-perfect marriage. When people started to jokingly call her my "office wife," it made me uncomfortable.

There were moments when Janie reminded me of Annabelle. There was an easy way of talking to Janie, something I missed after Annabelle and I split up. It hurt like hell to think of her. I missed her for years. I put my fist through a perfectly good door in my old flat weeks after I moved in, still resentful. I also sobbed like a baby one night after getting rat-arsed in a London pub. It took a good year for me to function like a normal person.

As the plane started to descend, I could see Baltimore, its

skyline, its harbor. It was a smooth ride. The plane was going to touch American soil, and I was about to begin anew, back at home, without a clue of how it would go or how I would begin.

* * *

My mother hugged me and kissed both my cheeks.

"Oh, Michael! We're so happy to see you and glad you are home!" My dad shook my hand and then pulled me close for a hug.

"Ciao, Michael!" my father said.

"Glad to be home," I said. "Let's go down to baggage claim. I can't wait to get to your house."

It was good to see them. My mother looked well. She had been on another one of her diets, but actually looked like she'd lost about ten pounds. My dad was always in shape, addicted to early morning workouts and biking. I hadn't seen my dad in a while, but for the first time, I noticed myself in him. We shared similar dark hair, though his was graying, and mine, for the most part, was still dark brown, almost black. We both had olive skin, and our slender builds also resembled one another. I didn't look like my mother at all. Her skin was fair and her hair was auburn. It wasn't natural, of course; she'd been dying it for years. She was curvy and had the most youthful, manicured hands.

It was four in the afternoon when we arrived; a perfectly gray November sky graced the landscape, and the chill of autumn was in the air. Autumn was my favorite season. Some might say it prepared us for winter, a time to sleep and become rejuvenated for spring, and that fall was what happened before things died. I never felt that way about it. It always felt refreshing after the hot summers and the humidity. Fall came before the frosts and snow and that merry holiday, Christmas, which, as Dickens wrote, was the season of charity and forgiveness.

When I first came to London, catatonic and broken, I walked around aimlessly like a robot. When September and October came, I began to feel the healing air, the crisp fall breeze and the energy of the season. I walked everywhere. Walks through Hyde Park helped me leave a lot of crap behind. Fall doesn't always mean the end of something. In fact, I wanted to believe it meant a new beginning.

* * *

When I opened my eyes, I heard the sound of raking of leaves coming from below my window. My father was busy sorting them into two very large piles. My mother brought the green trash bags out to him. I could hear their conversation through the glass.

"I bet we'll fill twenty bags," he said to my mother.

"I think you're probably right," she said.

It was eleven thirty and I was shocked that I'd slept the morning away. We'd stayed up talking until after midnight, sharing some wine with the television on for background noise. When I hit the pillow, I hit it hard. I don't remember the last thought I had before sleep.

The sun was shining, and it looked as if they picked the perfect day to work outside. I got dressed and had good intentions to help out. I had packed an old pair of jeans and a t-shirt. My father kept work boots in the garage, so I figured I'd borrow a pair of his. I hadn't shaved in two days, and the stubble on my face was pretty thick. I decided to shower after the yard work was completed.

The downstairs smelled like Maxwell House coffee; my mother

typically let the pot stay on all day and replenished it as needed. I poured myself a cup and stepped out onto the fieldstone patio in my socks.

"Morning," I shouted to them.

My mother walked over and gave me a squeeze. I saw the tree in the back of the yard. It sat at the edge of the property just before the yard dipped down towards to the water. I tried to ignore it. It was much bigger than it used to be.

"Got yourself some coffee, I see. Dad went out earlier and picked up some fresh pastries."

"I thought I could offer my services out here," I said, though I was instantly reminded of the pastry shop and my mouth began to water.

"Sure, but you need to eat."

She placed a sfogliatella on my plate. It looked amazing with its flakes, perfect triangular form, and powdered sugar. There were no Italian pastry shops anywhere near my flat. In fact, I hadn't had a good Italian meal in months. The last one I remembered was at Sciue Sciue in West Brompton. A group of us from *The Times* went out to celebrate Janie's birthday. The food was delicious, but it was the red wine I remembered from that night. Lots of wine flowing in and out of tall wine glasses. Janie was the life of the party, as she made sure no one went thirsty.

"Is this from Mrs. Marco's bakery?"

"Yes," my mother said.

"Are you all on speaking terms now?"

My mother nodded.

After all that catch-up talk last night, my mother had kept this from me. I didn't know she and Donna had let go of the past. Not that I ever thought cutting ties was the mature thing to do. I never wanted my family and Annabelle's family to have a cold war.

"How did that happen?" I asked. It was all very curious.

"Donna had cancer," my mother started. "When she was ill, I called Gil and asked him if she would see me and if I could help in any way. Things got better for us all then. When you and Annabelle, well, you know, it just never was the same for the four of us."

I looked at her as she told the story. "I know. I guess I'm just surprised you never told me she was sick. But she's okay now?"

"Yes, when they found the cancer, she was in stage two, but the chemo made her weak. She's been back at work full-time for a while now. She's doing rather well."

"And your friendship?"

"Good, Michael. It's good. I really missed them over the years, but so much time's gone by and you were with Lisbeth, and Annabelle was with someone, so time healed that wound for us."

Before I knew it, as riveted as I was with the discussion of the Marcos and the salvaged friendship, my sfogliatella was gone. I guess it was a good sign that I could eat through talk of that family. I wiped my face with a napkin, and saw my mother smiling at me.

"I guess you didn't like it," she joked. I nodded, sipped my coffee.

"Well, bugger, Mom, I guess I better just ask the question now and get it over with. What's the story with Annabelle? Have you seen her?"

"Yes. I see her occasionally. I saw her at the hospital when Donna was ill. She practically lived there and then even moved back home temporarily to take care of her with Gil. In fact, I saw her a few days ago when she picked Donna and Gil up from the airport. I think she's well. She's teaching at the college."

"Where does she live?" I asked, assuming she was going to say Baltimore with that guy she'd been living with for a while.

"She told me she bought a condo on Spa Creek. She lives by herself."

The coffee maker quieted after producing its full pot, and my mother poured me a second cup and passed the Half-and-Half. I wished she hadn't told me the last part. I hated that I wished she hadn't told me, too. I didn't want to be disturbed by anything. I promised myself not to allow that crap to affect me.

"Well, I better help Dad with the leaves," I said as I stepped outside into air as therapeutic as a shrink, as welcoming as a new day.

* * *

After we finished raking and bagging late in the afternoon, I had a beer with my dad. He asked me if I wanted to help get the boat to the marina for the winter. I never said no to a boat ride, and as it was nearing Thanksgiving, he was probably right to tuck her away until spring. He still loved the *The Lady L II*. She replaced the original *Lady L* when she went into retirement after my first year in London. She was named after his own Italian father's favorite movie, which happened to star my father's favorite actress of all time, Sophia Loren.

"Now there's a dynamo," he said every time he saw her on the screen. "I don't need any of these young, skinny actresses when I can look at her."

At least he had good taste in screen goddesses, which was more than I could say for his taste in ostentatious boats. His 42-ft Sea Ray was gorgeous, but I preferred smaller cuddy cabins.

The original *Lady L* was more to my liking. She was a 28-foot cuddy with lots of speed, and was the perfect boat for waterskiing. I loved boats. In fact, in high school I worked at the Yacht Club and was one of the jack-of-all-trades at the marina. I waited tables, cleaned boats, and pumped gasoline for customers at the dock.

"So, when are you supposed to head to New York for that interview?" my father asked as he poured himself another glass of wine, or, as he still called it by its Italian word, "vino." I sometimes regretted that I never learned the language. My father and late grandfather always spoke Italian to each other, but they never spoke it to me. I could only decipher words here and there.

"Next Tuesday," I said. "I'll go up and back the same day to avoid the Wednesday Thanksgiving crowds on the train."

"Good idea," he said. "Is this the job you want?"

"So far, I think it is. I've always wanted to work for a publishing house."

"What about your writing?" my father asked.

"I'll keep at it, Dad," I said. "Maybe I'll make some connections, but I've got to make a living."

"You've got a point there, son. Any word on the book?"

"No word either way, so hopefully it's not dead yet."

My father was a successful accountant. He worked for a firm in Washington, and after two years with the Army, attended George Washington University. He had cut out a niche for himself, and the boat was his reward for all his long hours and hard work.

"You boys ready?" my mother called.

"Guess I better turn the grill on for her," he said. My mother and father were the only people I knew who barbecued when there were icicles hanging off the roof and the ground was covered in two feet of snow.

"No Italian meal tonight?" I called back to her.

"No, that's for tomorrow. Baked ziti," she said.

"I think I'll take a walk down to the pier before I shower up," I said.

I hadn't been down to the pier in years. It used to be my favorite spot. If you walked down the dirt path, half covered with vines, you could get there faster than taking the little road. It had become chillier as the day wore on, but I was used to the dreary London weather. The warmth of the sun, even as it neared dusk, was keeping me from being cold. The view of Annapolis disappeared for a minute as I walked along behind the trees. When I came out of the brush at the bottom, the view was back. There it was—the Naval Academy and the wooden dome of the State House were directly across the way. I missed this place, the serenity of it. The river was peaceful. Even during the more vicious storms, the river was never a threat, and though it led to the Chesapeake Bay in the distance, its sound was calming. It was just as it always had been.

I took a deep breath and stretched my neck and arms. They were tired from raking. It was eerie being back. For a moment I wondered if I were off my trolley to have moved home. There were no taxicabs honking their horns, no constant hum of cars whizzing by, no inordinate number of people on the streets. I was back in my city, the place where I grew up, and then I realized it felt oddly comfortable, like wearing an old coat or reclining in a favorite chair. I couldn't say how long I'd be around; perhaps I was just passing through. Would it be New York, Annapolis, or some other place that would become my home? I honestly had no idea. I had loved living in New York and would probably love it again. Nonetheless, as I stood there, I embraced the quiet that surrounded me. It was a welcome change from the constant energy of my last ten years.

When I said goodbye so many years ago, it wasn't just because Annabelle left me, but also because I wasn't going to give up on the adventure we'd planned together. I was going to study abroad and was determined not to lose sight of that. I wanted to be in London, and though Annabelle had chosen not to be with me— sharing the experience, sharing the ride—the ride turned out to be okay in the end, even if I had done it alone. I wondered how her ride had treated her.

We stood in this very place the day I was accepted to the University of London. She reached up to hug me, her arms around me. I remembered looking into her eyes, her brown hair cascading past her shoulders, the faint smell of her perfume on her neck, wanting things to stay the same, yet knowing our lives were about to change. At the time, I just didn't know they'd change so drastically. That was a lifetime ago.

It's curious what time does to a person. I looked around, breathed in the smell of the river. I was back.

A wave hit the dock and splashed my shoe. In the distance, I watched a sailboat glide by, its sail tall and commanding. Its captain waved to me from the helm. I raised my hand and waved back. From somewhere deep down in my core, I felt a pang of happiness.

Part Two

1982-1987

Annabelle

My parents and their best friends, the Contellis, were out to
dinner and a late movie. I'd been to the football game, but my best
friend Andie had gone home to bed. She had a field hockey game
the next morning. I flopped on my bed, put one of my mix cassettes
in, and grabbed a *Seventeen* magazine. It came in the mail a couple
of days ago and I hadn't had a chance to read it. It was ironic that
I'd subscribed to this publication for years and that I was finally
the same age as the title—seventeen, but about to turn eighteen. I'd
already applied to college and was beginning to feel like this senior
year was going to be about waiting. Waiting to finish high school.
Waiting to go to college. I knew I wanted to be an English major;
it was always my favorite subject and I loved literature. I'd read
magazines, newspapers, books—you name it. I lived for summers
because I could catch up on novels I didn't get a chance to read
during the school year when I was too focused on earning good
grades.

I hadn't eaten at the game and I hadn't participated, either. Last
week during cheerleading practice, I had poorly executed a round-
off-back-handspring, and landed on my foot the wrong way, in a
sideways sort of position. The sprain was enough for the doctors
to implore me to keep off it for three to four weeks, so cheerleading was out of the question. I'd quickly become tired of hobbling
around with a tightly wrapped bandage and foot brace and thought
I could ditch the crutches by putting the weight on my toes as I
arched my feet up when I walked. I thought my mother was going

to kill me for not using the crutches. "You're going to do permanent damage, Annabelle," she said, "and you won't be happy about that later in life." My mother was convinced that the things we do now, every little thing, can have a negative impact on us at some later date.

I slowly made it to the stairs, dragging my sprained ankle behind me, my mother's words echoing in my head. I sat down and glided my way to the bottom. Then I hopped on one foot to the kitchen and began to raid the refrigerator for something that interested me. There was leftover chicken ragu wrapped nicely in a square Pyrex dish. As I began to unwrap the dish, I heard a sound. It was a strange, loud, growling sound. I shimmied over to the window to hear it better. It sounded like it was coming from the side yard. Whatever it was, it was constant and unsettling. I hadn't ever heard a sound like that before.

Thinking that maybe my parents were hanging out over at the Contellis' house, I dialed their number. After the fourth ring, I almost hung up, but an out-of-breath Michael answered.

"Hello?"

"Hi, Michael. It's Annabelle. Are my parents there?"

"No, they haven't gotten home yet," he said. "I thought you might have gone out after the game."

"I was at the game, but I just got home. I was calling because there's a strange noise coming from outside. Can you hear it?"

He became quiet for a second.

"What is it?"

"I don't know. It sounds weird. Can you hear it?"

"No, but maybe if I step out on the patio I can. Wait a minute."

Again, he disappeared. He must have dropped the phone because I heard a thud as it hit the hardwood floor. About a minute later, he picked it up.

"I did hear something weird. Want me to come over? I'll grab a flashlight and be right there. Hang tight."

"Okay," I said, "Come to the back door. I'll open it."

He didn't have to worry about me running anywhere, not with my foot in this still-swollen state. I unlocked the door, and within minutes, could see him traipsing through his backyard and into mine, flashlight bobbing in one hand. He shined it through the doorway and right into my eyes.

"Oh, sorry about that," he said, as I shielded the light with my hand. "I do hear it. I think I might know what it is. You want to come outside?"

"No, I better stay here, unless you want to help me walk," I said, pointing to my injury. "It's really swollen from standing on it a lot today."

"Let me have a look and I'll be right back."

With that, he began searching around the yard. He seemed to be taking it very seriously, which pleased me because had he not been home, I don't know what I would have done. The noise was definitely eerie.

He reappeared, this time, lowering the flashlight down to the ground. "Do you have a broom? And maybe pliers?"

I opened the door and told him where they were in the garage. "What is it?"

"A possum is caught in the chicken wire around the garden. I may be able to get it out. Can I wear these garden gloves?"

"Sure," I said. "I want to come with you."

"Grab my arm," he said, and I did.

With Michael's flashlight as our guide, we made it out to the garden, and there was the possum, scared and stuck. His mouth was open, and he was shrieking, but it came out more like a growl and a hiss.

"I'm going to try just gently wiggling the wire with the broom so I don't scare him more than he already is. I may be able to loosen it."

"Is he bleeding?" I asked, now worried about the little creature.

"No, well, maybe just a bit. It's not bad from what I can see in the dark."

Michael jiggled the chicken wire fence with the broom, but the possum still was scrambling to get out, his screech silenced by our presence. Michael grabbed the pliers and pulled the top part of the wire. Still nothing. The possum was caught.

"What if you bend the opposite sides outward and I pull the top part. Do you think that would work?"

"Maybe," he said. "Let's try."

We tried that, but to no avail. "Let me see the broom again. I'm going to wiggle this part one more time," he said.

And with that, the little possum was freed. It gave out a final cry of relief, and scurried back to the brush, and hopefully to a family that was waiting for him.

Michael looked at me, his dark eyes wide, his flashlight still our only source of light besides the patio lights in the distance. I gave a laugh, and said, "Whew, that was something," and then he moved close to me so he could help me back to my house. I hopped on one foot up to the concrete patio.

"Thanks for coming over. I would have been freaked out if you hadn't been home."

"I can understand why," he said. "Wanna have a beer with me? I've got a little stash out in the shed. They might be a little warm, but a beer's a beer."

This was an odd proposition coming from Michael, my neighbor since we were both five, the son of my parents' best friends. He and I had always been friendly because we had no choice; we were often thrown together for various functions. It wasn't unusual for us to have conversations around our families, but at school we rarely communicated at all. He must have seen the quizzical look on my face, because he pulled out the patio chair and told me to sit. "Wait here for a minute, and I'll be right back," he said.

It was difficult to say no to him, because he was probably one of the nicest boys I knew. He wasn't pompous and arrogant like other boys. He didn't play on the football team, but rather on the golf team, and his grades were stellar. And so, that night, I didn't say no to him. Instead, I waited on that patio chair for what seemed like ten minutes, until he appeared with a wheelbarrow draped with a blanket.

"What is that?" I asked.

"Get in," he said.

"In that?"

"Am I holding something else for you to get into?" he shrugged.

He helped me turn around and I sunk my butt down. I was laughing. This was hilarious. "Lift your feet up a little," he commanded.

He wheeled me over to his back yard where he had arranged a little picnic under the mimosa tree that ironically we had given his family as a gift for their one-year anniversary in their home. It was a lovely tree with a large canopy, though its leaves were tucked in for sleep. It still had some pink blossoms, even in the late summer, though they were not as vibrant as they once were. There was a six-pack of Bud on the blanket and Doritos and salsa in the jar. The flashlight was on and sitting on the blanket like a candle. It was pretty cool.

"Come on," he said, "come hang with me. I've got nothing to do and apparently neither do you now that the possum has left you."

"You mean now that we have saved the possum from death in a vegetable garden."

"Correct," he said. "Come sit and put your leg up."

He took the blanket that was in the wheelbarrow and folded it up to form a pillow. "See," he said. "Foot goes here."

He popped open a Bud for me and then one for himself. I didn't like beer very much, but I didn't want to hurt his feelings, so I took a sip. We weren't legally supposed to drink alcohol at seventeen, and a lot of kids had been looking forward to their eighteenth birthdays until this year when Maryland law raised the drinking age to twenty-one. But kids still got their hands on beer and Boone's Farm, which I'd sworn off for all eternity after a crazy night and consumption of almost an entire bottle earlier in the summer.

Surprisingly, it was going down rather smoothly, and I'm not sure if it was because I was in unfamiliar territory alone with Michael or because I was extremely flattered by his attention and creativity. I'd never seen him quite so innovative and expressive. It was almost as if I were sitting under the tree with a whole new Michael.

"So, have you applied to any colleges yet?" he asked me.

"I have. All local ones. You?"

"Yeah, I have, too. I just sent one off to NYU, which is my first choice, Fordham University, and Columbia University. I hope I hear back soon."

"All of them in New York, right?"

"Yes. I want to be a journalist, at least that's what I think right now. Anyway, I love it here, don't get me wrong, but I figured it would be cool to live and go to college in New York. I don't think I could get bored there at all. Plenty of museums and sports to keep somebody happy along with school."

It was quiet for a minute, the chirping of the crickets taking center stage. The sky was clear; as we looked straight ahead, the stars were out and seemed to be winking at the river. "So how did you kill your foot again?" he asked.

"Stupid, really. I landed in the wrong position when I came out of a back-handspring. My foot was forced sideways."

"See? That's why I stick with golf. If you get hurt in golf, you deserve the injury."

That made me laugh. He was funny, but I already knew that about him. He always had a good sense of humor; there was a nice, easy way about him. My father perpetually raved about Michael. "Did you know Michael said this?" or "Did you know Michael won an award?" Blah, blah, blah. My dad adored him, and I always assumed it was because he never had a son of his own.

"So what are your big plans for senior year?" he asked.

"I don't think I have any big plans, but thanks for making me feel bad about it," I teased.

"How can you have no big plans? You've got to have big plans! This is your senior year of high school. It's never going to happen again in your life. You have to do something really fantastic, something memorable…something you can tell your kids about when you're old and gray." He took a swig, stretched out on the blanket as he turned to see my reaction, and waited. He was wearing blue jeans and a gray Naval Academy t-shirt. His flip-flops sat on the edge of the blanket. "Come on, you've got to come up with something."

"I don't know!" I said, laughing again. "What are your big plans? What will you tell your kids?"

"I couldn't tell you. I have absolutely no idea," he said.

"Oh, but you're pressing me to come up with something creative. Nice…"

"Well, I just think planning is important to the success of one's own life," he said. "That is, unless you want your parents to plan your whole life for you."

I laughed at him as he pontificated on life's big issues. "What are you saying?"

"I don't know. It just seems like our parents like to drive the bus, you know? They always seem to want to steer me in the direction they believe I should go." I couldn't have agreed with him more. I felt exactly the same way. He continued, "I mean, when have we ever been able to talk like this when they're around?"

"You are right," I said, feeling a little bit lighter in the head than when I had first rested on the blanket. "It's just how they are." We both thought about it and sipped our beers. "Speaking of our families, can you believe my family gave your family this tree? I mean, look at the size of it now. I remember us giving it to you and our dads digging the hole for it. Sometimes that feels like it was just yesterday. Other times, it feels like it was a lifetime ago," I said.

He was watching me intently, listening to my words, my thoughts. The moon had just appeared over the Severn, and I looked over at him that night and examined his wavy dark hair, his brown, big eyes, and his nice build. Had I lived next door to him all these years and never noticed him before? Or were the beers I'd been drinking affecting my perceptions?

He sat up and moved his body closer to mine, the two of us

sitting with our feet outstretched, mine on the makeshift pillow, his extended out, his hip and hand brushing up against me.

"I have an idea of how we can make senior year memorable," he said.

"Yeah?"

"Come with me out on the boat tomorrow, just you and me. Our parents are going to the Navy Football game. We won't tell anyone, and you and I can take her out. What do you say?"

"And my foot?" I asked.

"It's welcome to come too," he said.

* * *

I went to bed that night strangely unsettled, but intrigued by Michael's idea. And the irony was, I had no idea what it meant or if he had any romantic intentions. Our outing under the mimosa tree had ended amicably. He had wheeled me home, just as I had arrived, teasing me all the way. At one point, he spun the wheelbarrow around and around, and I had trouble catching my breath through the laughter that yielded a pretty intense bellyache and a little bit of the spins. I felt the beer swishing in my stomach.

As I got ready for bed, I heard my parents slip in through the garage door, tiptoeing up the stairs as if they were afraid to wake me. They were whispering to each other to be quiet, which made me giggle.

I stared at the ceiling watching the fan turn round and round. The light from the back patio lit my room. I was far from tired. My adrenaline seemed to be pumping. This was ludicrous, I thought. We've known each other for twelve plus years. What is happening here?

I tried to sleep, but I found myself restless. Something odd was happening, and I was trying to put my finger on it: I'd never really had this type of attention paid to me by a boy before. Sure, there were the occasional flirtations and I had gone to the junior prom with Nick Arnold, but I'd never had a guy go out of his way for me. And though it was not an official date—our strange intimacy having occurred thanks to a trapped possum—it had all the makings of a date.

I sat up and slapped myself. What are you thinking? I said out loud. This is Michael Contelli we are talking about! He is my neighbor, my friend, son of my parents' best friends.

No. This cannot be, I told myself, and then tried again to go to sleep. Sometime around three-thirty in the morning I stopped seeing the clock.

* * *

"Don't forget to let the dog out," my mother said, as she kissed me goodbye, her coral lipstick leaving a mark on my face.

"I won't," I said. "I'll do it now."

"And if you get a chance, can you pick up the clothes that are littered all over the floor of your room?" my father asked.

I was eager for them to leave and they seemed to be dawdling, adjusting their Navy jerseys, packing their tailgate picnic table and chairs, and putting their beer on ice.

"What are you going to do today?" they asked as they shoved a cooler in the trunk of their Buick. "Stuff," I said. "Take care of the dog. Clean my room. Go to the library to start my research project for botany."

"Sounds like a full day!" my dad exclaimed, shutting the trunk and clapping his hands. "We'll be screaming in the stands."

"Is that crazy lady still there?" I used to go with them to Navy games, but stopped attending a couple of years ago when I became busier at school and with my friends.

"What crazy lady?"

"You know, the one with the cheer? That stupid one that goes 'retard them, retard them, make them relinquish the ball!' That lady."

"Yes, she's still there and it's not stupid. It's an alliteration cheer, sweetie," my mother said, giving me a quick peck on the forehead.

"Duh," I said, as I watched them get into the car and pull away. I hobbled upstairs to change into something appropriate for a boat ride in late September.

* * *

"What do you have in that basket?" he asked me when he saw me hobbling his way. "Need a hand?"

"Sandwiches and brownies."

"Nice idea," he said.

He took the picnic basket and extended his arm to me as we made our way down the path to the boat dock. The *Lady L* appeared ready to ride, her cover off, her blower on. Michael smelled like Old Spice, a scent my nose was familiar with since my father used the aftershave as well. He looked freshly shaven because there was a little nick on the side of his face, a little remnant of toilet paper stuck to his cheek. I didn't have the heart to tell him he'd forgotten to remove it.

He was wearing a gray long-sleeved tee shirt, jeans, and flip-flops, his lean body readying the boat for departure.

"Can I help?" I asked him, feeling worthless.

"I can't have my first-mate get hurt. I'll undo the lines and you can throw them on the dock when we take off," he said.

I watched him work, easing us out of the boat slip and into the river. I threw the rear lines up to the dock and they actually caught. In minutes, we would be cruising at high speed, the wind against our faces, the wake of our boat rippling the river. My dad's boat wasn't as nice as this one; this one was top notch. The engine was much quieter than ours, which made it feel smoother. Michael was behind the wheel and motioned for me to move up next to him. I hopped over and sat down. The smell of the water and the warmth of the sun were invigorating. He looked at me and smiled.

"Weird, huh?" he shouted into the wind.

"Yeah?" I shouted back, looking at him, raising my eyebrows in question.

"We've never done this before," he said, holding his free arm up against the strength of the wind. "I love this feeling!"

His enthusiasm for it had me smiling. We'd never talked about boating before. My hair was whipping in the wind, our sunglasses reflecting the brightness of the sun; we waved to other boaters as they passed, their wake and our wake melding into the river's own lullaby.

We cruised the river for a while and then we rode over to one of the smaller creeks where we threw over the anchor, turned up the little transistor radio, and opened up the picnic lunch. It was warm for September, but not hot. There had been little rain this year, and the grass had been burned out in places. But out on the water, with views of waterfront properties and the sound of birds overhead, these imperfections could not be seen. The water was calm and the rays of the sun glistened off the still water. Boater traffic was light because only the hardcore enthusiasts kept their boats in the water long after summer vacations. Our two families usually left the boats in until late fall or early winter, once the frosts came and stayed.

I propped my foot up on the seat across from me and opened the tabs of our Cokes. Neither one of us said much. I wasn't sure if it was tension or comfort. I finally broke the quiet.

"I'm glad you asked me out on the boat today, Michael. Otherwise, I'd be at the library researching my botany project."

"But you still have to do it, right?"

"Yes," I said, "but it can wait until tomorrow."

"You should think about going to college in New York," he said, taking a bite of his sandwich.

"I should?"

"Yeah. Don't you think it would be cool to live in New York City?"

"Maybe."

"What do you mean, maybe? It's the greatest city on earth, though I haven't been to many of the big cities around the world. But it's the Big Apple. What do you want to study in college?"

"English."

"Well, there you go. You can study English in New York."

I smiled at him while he was talking. He probably just wanted someone he knew to go there with him so that he could have a friend in a city of eight million people.

"I'll think about it," I said, "but I already got an acceptance here and maybe a scholarship."

"Well, you never know until you try," he said.

We talked about school for a while, and Mrs. Moreau, our

French teacher. She could never get anyone's name right; she messed them up all the time because we had to choose a French name for class and then she'd confuse the French name with our real name. It was hilarious.

When we finished our sandwiches, he came and sat next to me on the rear bench, and asked me how my foot was feeling. He picked it up gently and put it on his lap with ease, and I stretched out, my back leaning up against the upholstered bench. Nothing about this gesture felt odd. In fact, it felt unusually comfortable.

"Still weird, right?" He stared at me, smiling, waiting for an answer.

His honesty caught me off guard, but that was Michael. Always direct. He didn't mince words. As long as I'd known him, he was always a straight shooter.

I answered. "Not really."

"Good, because I like spending time with you."

"Well, I like spending time with you too. I mean, we do it a lot with our folks."

"Yes, I know. That's the point. It's always with our families," he said almost regretfully. "Sometimes it's strange, you know?"

"What? That we never really talk unless our parents are around?"

He nodded. "It's too bad, isn't it?"

"Yeah, too bad," I found myself repeating, without realizing or thinking about it. I watched him for a minute. He started to caress my good foot, his hand and thumb rubbing across the top of it, gently, sweetly. Somewhere between last night and this pure gesture of affection, I felt something flutter within me. Something that seemed beyond words, like it's always been there, brewing, I thought. And likewise, I believe it was then, when his eyes twinkled in the sunlight as his boat floated in the river, that I realized something that may have been in front of my face for a very long time: Michael may have loved me.

* * *

When we made our way off the boat and up to the house, empty picnic basket in hand, Michael helped me hobble back to my front door. We stood there for a moment, a little uneasy, not sure as to how to say goodbye. He touched the side of my arm and looked at me in the eyes.

"So that was okay, right? All good?" he said, wanting and needing me to confirm that we hadn't lost anything, but rather gained something during the day together.

"No," I said, feeling unusually flirtatious. "It was better than okay."

He looked surprised for a second, then his smile took over his face. I'll remember that look for as long as I live.

"I'm glad," he said, and his hand moved from my upper arm, down past my elbow to my hand, which he took in his own and brought to his lips. He kissed the top of it. I liked the way his warm, wet lips felt on my skin.

"Should we do this again?" he asked. I nodded.

"Okay, then, we'll figure out another time," he said.

He turned toward his house, his shoulder square and his posture perfect, and walked away from me. I let him take about twenty steps.

"Michael—" I found myself shouting, and then, doing the best run-shuffle I could manage, ignoring the throbbing in my ankle, ran to him. He turned, and it was I—I who reached for him and kissed him for the very first time. I felt a sensation in my legs I hadn't yet felt in my seventeen years; they went weak and wobbly, and Michael, his mouth pressed against mine, seemed to catch me. His hands were holding my face, and I don't know if I breathed at all in the time we stood there, melding into each other. However, I was certain of one thing: the presence of an aching pain from my foot was absent, and I felt only heat and tasted the warmth of love for the first time on that September day.

* * *

We started spending a lot of time together after that, and things began to change for us. We started to seek each other out instead of waiting for a push from our parents, a force that had always been omnipresent, though they'd probably say it wasn't apparent. There were countless little innuendos about the two of us prior to that evening, like when your mother insists you try the spinach with the garlic and onions, but you're pretty sure you don't want something distasteful forced down your throat. At one point, I overheard a conversation between my mother and Carol when they were having coffee. I heard our names uttered, and when I opened the cabinet looking for a snack, they became mute. Then there was the time in tenth grade when Michael didn't have a date to Homecoming and my mother asked me if I would go with him. Another boy, Roy Woods, had already asked me and I'd accepted, so I told my mother I couldn't go with Michael.

"That's a shame," my mother had said. "Michael's such a sweet boy. And always so polite and nice. You two would make an attractive couple."

"True," I said, "but I'm going with Roy."

Homecoming with Roy was the worst night of my life. He tried way too hard to stick his tongue in my mouth and attempted many times to rub his hands and body against my breasts.

I later regretted telling my mother I didn't want to go with Michael.

But the night beneath the mimosa tree changed everything. We would ride the bus together to school or catch a ride with each other if we drove to school; we would eat lunch together in the cafeteria; we would meet at the library to study. There were the little things at first, and then there were our secret meetings and the lies we began to tell.

Sometimes we'd meet under the tree, sneaking outside after our parents had gone to bed, or go down to the river and hang out on the docks, telling our parents we were with our friends, but really just trying to find a way to be together without anyone else knowing. It became a game to see if we'd get caught, but we never did. Either that or our parents never let us know they knew.

* * *

We finally had to come clean in the spring, and as we neared graduation, we decided to go public with our decision to attend prom together. It was quite a shock to those who knew us, because we had been clandestine about our relationship. Our friends were utterly surprised, especially Andie.

"Why would you keep it a secret? Don't you trust me?" she asked, her feelings hurt.

"You don't get it, Andie," I said. "We really kept it quiet because of our parents. You know, they've been subtly pushing us together for years. We've always felt pressure from them. And then we just happened to spend time together without their insistence and it just happened. Honestly, I didn't keep it from you on purpose."

Try as I might to make her understand, it took her weeks to get over my big cover up. Our parents, on the other hand, couldn't have been happier.

"It's kismet," my mother had said. "We all knew it would happen."

When the prom came along, my mother, Michael's mother, and our fathers all chimed in on the action, snapping photographs, presenting flowers, arranging a limo. Honestly, the wedding of Princess Di and Prince Charles paled in comparison to the fuss that occurred over our prom date.

When college became the topic of everyday conversation, we debated a lot. Michael was determined to go to New York and study there, but I had been accepted at Maryland on a scholarship and I was really proud of that. Despite the sound reasoning to attend Maryland, and when they all knew we were serious about each other, my father offered to send me to college in New York so that Michael and I would be together, but I was not inclined to do so, no matter how kind the offer. Plus, I didn't have the burning desire at the time to live in New York. I must have said a hundred times to Michael that if our relationship were strong enough, it would survive the distance and the parental interference.

"Are you sure I can't convince you to come?" Michael said to me one night as we were sitting on the dock making a lame attempt at crabbing.

"We've been over this a thousand times. You go to New York and I promise to visit. It's only a three-hour car ride," I said.

"Without traffic," he moaned.

I hated disappointing him. He and I had grown extremely close over the last eight months. I was probably closer to him than I'd been with anyone before. His downturned mouth said everything.

"Look," I said. "We've been friends for a long time. We're going to be fine."

He scratched his hair, looked away, and then he spoke.

"Yes, but things are different now."

* * *

When Michael was accepted to New York University, the decision factor was over. We had both chosen our respective colleges and the agonizing ended. It was when we made this decision that our relationship changed again. I think part of the growth of our love was due to our decision to commit to each other. I knew how much I loved him, and I knew how much he loved me. I wanted our relationship to work, evolve, and grow.

Michael wanted to make sure that a career in journalism was the right path for him. He had such amazing talents. He could paint, illustrate, write, and was good with people, so his choices seemed limitless. I jokingly called him my "Leonardo," my "Renaissance Man." One lazy summer afternoon, days before we were to leave for college, he sketched me sitting on the dock at the river's edge. There was an unusual breeze blowing, as if a storm were brewing in the distance.

"Move that hair away from your chin," he commanded. "I can't see your face."

"Okay," I said. I had been sitting in one position for far longer than anyone should have to sit, the tilt of my head causing a crick in my neck.

"You're still moving," he said.

"I know! Do you have any idea how hard it is to stay in one position this long! I don't know how kings and queens posed for hours on end while their portraits were being completed!"

"It's called patience, sweetheart. You cannot rush an artist," he teased, giving me a sheepish grin. "Not if it's to be done the right way."

That sketch was one of the most treasured items I owned. He did something magical with his brushes on that canvas that made me look exotic and beautiful. I never saw myself that way.

Saying goodbye to him that first time wasn't easy. I didn't want it to become melodramatic in the driveway, so I hurried over as his parents were putting the last few items in the car to drive him to New York. We stepped aside for a little privacy.

I handed him a basket of things I'd put together: a little clock radio, a box of some love notes I'd been writing all summer, three bags of M&Ms, some magazines, a photograph of the two of us in a frame from a recent party, and a mix tape of our favorite songs.

"What's this?" he asked.

"Things to remind you," I said. I was having more trouble with the reality that he was leaving than I thought I would. "Just remember…" my voice started to crack.

"I know," he said, smirking. "You love me."

I gave him a little smack on the arm, and then we both laughed, hugged each other, kissed, and said our first of many goodbyes we faced over the course of our college years.

* * *

After a semester at NYU, Michael zeroed in on journalism and stuck with it. It seemed he wasn't convinced he could make a living sketching, no matter how talented an artist he was.

In the end, being apart wasn't too bad; we got used to the back and forth travel from Maryland to New York. We convinced ourselves that we could overcome the separation, and he still tried every now and then to get me to transfer. I never wanted to. As much as my parents are sweet and caring, I was dying to feel some independence from everyone. Had I gone to New York, Michael would have kept me from being independent because, despite his good intentions, I would have done things he wanted me to do. I lived on campus at Maryland, so I had a little bit of freedom from my family.

Several of my friends were involved in activities on campus, and I joined some clubs too. I worked part-time in the admissions office and earned extra cash. Three fellow English majors and I spent countless hours in the library during the week, studying everything from Shakespeare to children's literature, but honestly, most of my time was spent writing papers. I tried to get as much completed during the week as I could, and then I'd bring whatever reading remained on the train with me.

Our compromise, therefore, came mostly in the form of Amtrak, as Michael and I would visit each other as often as we could. What I did gain from the relationship in the end, besides a sense of commitment and resounding love for someone, was a growing affinity for New York.

I remember when Michael took me to the top of the World Trade Center; I could actually feel the building swaying. We stepped outside to see the view—the Brooklyn Bridge, the Statue of Liberty, Manhattan and all its glory—with flyaway hair outside on the observatory, he stood behind me, his arms around my waist as we breathed in the air. "Isn't this amazing?" he said, as he kissed me up there in the sky.

I often brought my books with me to study and we'd spend time in the library, particularly the New York Public Library. We didn't have to talk; just being together, working side by side, was all we needed. However, there were times when I needed his help.

"What do you think I'm supposed to do here?" I'd ask him, pointing to a problem in the textbook. I was forced to take statistics—a class I abhorred—and he'd become frustrated with me, laughing at my ineptitude.

"You don't want to get it, do you? It's as plain as day! This is how you find the mode," he'd say, working the problem out on paper for me. Despite his extreme patience with me, sometimes I still couldn't grasp it.

"But why would I *want* to find the mode? When am I ever going to actually need to find the mode in my life?"

"You're impossible," he'd say, smirking at me, his eyes glistening. "You want to find the mode, because if you don't find it and you don't know how to find it, you will fail the class."

Needless to say, I did learn how to find the mode, the median, and the mean, primarily because he took the time to help me. Math was never my strong suit, but I passed the class thanks to him.

During the second semester of Michael's sophomore year, he started working on NYU's newspaper. I admired him for his dedication to it; he seemed to love it. I became involved with Maryland's literary journal and our lives became busier. Despite our somewhat exasperating college schedules, we always found time for each other. Plus, we spent countless hours of quality time together during breaks, and we made the most of our summers and

our free time. That's why sometimes it's just impossible to compre-
hend what I did to him. To us.

I honestly don't know what happened to me. I truly loved him.
More than anyone will ever know.

* * *

It was the Saturday morning before Halloween during my
senior year. I came home for the weekend to work on a two-part
capstone project, and wanted to have peace to write. However,
before I locked myself in my room with my typewriter, I helped
my mother put the finishing touches on my parents' costumes for
the neighborhood party. My mother was going to be Cher, and my
father, Sonny Bono.

"Why couldn't we have gone as Captain Stubing and Julie Mc-
Coy?" my mother whined. "We could have borrowed Cheryl's and
Dan's costumes. This Cher wig is absolutely ridiculous and that
Sonny wig isn't too great either, dear."

"I am not going to be the captain," he said. "You're lucky I'm
even dressing up at all. Hateful holiday! Teaching kids to beg for
candy. My parents didn't come to this country so I could teach my
child to be a beggar."

We'd heard this rant many times before, and I often wondered
if he still considered me a child of trick-or-treat age who would actually go door-to-door. My mother's been with him long enough to
know how to handle it. She rolled her eyes and ignored his antics,
as she so often did.

Carol walked in the door without knocking, calling "Ciao,
friends!" in her high-pitched voice.

She stopped abruptly when she saw me sitting at the kitchen

table, thread and needle in my hand, my father standing beside me, as I put the fringe on his costume.

"Oh—hello, Annabelle. I didn't expect to see you here. Why aren't you in New York with Michael?" She certainly never beat around the bush.

"Michael had a newspaper staff dinner tonight," I said.

"But everything's okay with you two, right?" she persisted.

"Yes, fine," I said, watching my mother and Carol exchange concerned glances.

"Ouch," my father said, when I accidentally stuck him with the needle. "Careful, there. I'd like to keep that leg if you don't mind."

I giggled. My father might gripe about this silly holiday, but he always retained his sense of humor.

My mother couldn't let it go once Carol got the ball rolling. "Is there something you're not telling us, honey?"

"No." I was determined not to play at their games.

"Are you positive?"

"I'm positive," I said. "He's busy. I'm busy. Don't you guys get that we're in college—and seniors! It gets busier and harder, you know."

"Oh, sure," Carol said. "I know. Michael tells me all the time how busy he is. But he said you two haven't seen each other in three weeks."

Could that be right? I thought. I hadn't been counting.

"Wow," I said. "I wasn't really keeping track."

I finished up my dad's stitches and told him to take off the groovy top. Just we three ladies were left in the kitchen.

"You know you can talk to us if there's something wrong," my mother said.

"Oh my God!" I shouted. "There's nothing wrong! We're just

swamped with schoolwork and extracurricular activities! Let it go!"

I walked out of the kitchen slamming the door behind me. I took a deep breath and inhaled the fresh air. I'd been inside too long. I'd only been home since last night, and I already needed a walk. I took myself for a good long one, allowing myself to be rained on by the fall foliage as I escaped briefly from parental claws and found peace in the restorative air.

* * *

During the last semester of our college days, I began to worry that I'd only been with Michael and no one else. My parents' involvement caused me to resent my relationship with Michael. When our parents talked about our future together, Michael would smile, but I became frustrated, nervous, and angry. When they would go on and on about what our kids might look like, I would have to leave the room.

I began to detest their meddling, as it grew layer by layer, like a stacked sandwich. As much as I loved Michael, my parents' strange push for us to be together was always there. Their interference was uninhibited. It was like being under a microscope. They were always around us, and I became uncomfortable in front of them. I viewed our relationship as one of those Victorian match-ups, where the parents decide whom you will marry based on certain requirements. I began to believe that our parents plotted our relationship from the day we met, at five, in the backyard, as we played on the swing set together.

One afternoon during spring break—engrossed in a novel and reclining on a lawn chair in my bikini, my body slathered with

Baby Oil—Mrs. Contelli walked over to say hi and have a little chat.

"Hello, Annabelle!" she said.

"Hi, Mrs. Contelli."

"Michael tells me you two aren't going to join us on Saturday for the neighborhood barbecue. You two never miss!"

"Yes, I know," I said, "but we've been invited to my friend's party in D.C., and I really feel I need to go."

"It's not often the neighbors get to see you two anymore," she persisted. "Don't you think you could stop by for a little while? You know how everyone loves to see you two."

My face felt hot, and I was pretty sure it wasn't due to the sun bearing down on me.

Later that day, in a moment of pure frustration, I said to Michael, "I'm so tired of being pushed! Why are our parents always in our shit?"

"What do you mean?" he asked.

"I feel like they try to manipulate us. That we're supposed to do what they want, when they want, and that, God forbid, if we weren't together, neither one of us would survive." It was just our luck that we were both only children and the product of Italian-Americans who loved the idea of keeping Italians in the family.

"What is that supposed to mean?" he asked. Is he living in a cocoon, I thought.

"Nothing, nothing…" He stared at me; I knew my words hurt. I tried to backtrack. "It's just that they're pushy. And we're always under a microscope. They act like we should just know that it is destiny that we're together. "

"Maybe it is," he said dejectedly.

I knew he was right, so I tried to calm down. My temper could often get the better of me.

"Yes, yes, I know," I said, utterly frustrated and wondering why Michael couldn't understand the microscope metaphor. "But doesn't their constant involvement bother you?"

"Yes, in a way it does, but then I think of you—of us—and I put it out of my head."

I let it go after that.

I should have opened up more to Michael. It would have been better for me to describe the interference and meddling I felt. And perhaps that is what comes with being an only child. I never believed I was meant to be an only child, and I guess I always assumed that I would have a brother or a sister at some point, but Sophia, my sister of two days, died of respiratory distress syndrome, and my mother swore she'd never go through that kind of heartbreak again. Italian women do not make promises that they cannot keep. For all of my mother's niceness, she was one stubborn woman. For whatever reason, the intensity of the focus on the two of us caused me to feel things I hadn't felt before, and instead of trusting Michael to be my best friend and the love of my life, I started keeping things to myself. These feelings festered, and I stewed in silence.

* * *

I had been accepted into the graduate program at University of Maryland for the fall, and though it was only May and graduation was a week away, I wanted to pursue this idea. I had made the final decision that I wanted to be a college professor.

Michael arrived home from NYU. His graduation was to take place two days before mine, and because of the excitement, all six of us went out to dinner to celebrate at Carroll's Creek Café.

When the appetizers arrived, three waiters gathered around the table with glasses of Champagne in each hand, and Michael got down on one knee. In a restaurant full of people, my parents with mile-wide smiles, his folks giddy and clapping, Michael pulled a diamond from his pocket. He knelt down in front of me.

"Annabelle—you are my soul mate and my best friend and I love you. Will you marry me?"

I said yes. I could not say no. How could I? The congratulations and clapping and celebration did not lend itself to saying no. He had caught me completely off-guard. He stood up and hugged me, kissed my hand, and placed the large diamond on my finger. I silently wondered if his parents had helped offset the cost of it.

In hindsight, I guess I always knew this was a possibility, but I had no idea it would come so soon. We were still so young. I'd become obsessed with the silly behavior my parents had exhibited, from rushing outside whenever we'd pull up in the car after being out of the house for a while, to inviting us to dinner or out for drinks or to Navy football games. Sometimes I scratched my head at the ease with which Michael could ignore it all.

The day after our college graduations, my mother handed me a book and phone numbers for wedding planners. She told me Carol had lots of ideas, and that we needed to start organizing our lists and select a date.

Later that night, Michael and I took a walk over the bridge into Annapolis by ourselves for a drink. I broached the subject.

"I think we should elope," I said.

"Elope?"

"Yes."

"What about our parents? They'd be so disappointed!" he said.

"I don't care, Michael," I found myself saying. "This is about us, not them. For once, let's make the most important day of our lives about us. We can have some sort of party or reception when we get back if they want. If you want to do this, let's do it secretly and make it our special wedding."

"Annabelle," he began, "it can't be just about us. This is a happy occasion and one they will want to share with us. We can't just cut them out of it. We can't do that. It's not nice, first of all, and second of all, I think you will regret it in the end."

"Okay, then," I succumbed, after thinking it through, "but I don't want a big wedding. I want a wedding on the beach in the Caribbean and they can come if they want!" I threw my arms around him. "How does that sound as a compromise? Just us—and them, of course—in the Bahamas, on the beach for our wedding. Because I have a feeling if we begin to plan one, it will be the wedding our mothers never had and will not reflect what either one of us wants."

"That sounds perfect," he said. And I could tell he was happy.

* * *

"What do you think about the two of us going to grad school in London?" he asked me one afternoon. "My friend Andrew's been accepted to a program and it might be great for us to get away. We can get jobs and a flat—you know that's what they call apartments there, right?—and go to grad school. And that will allow you to soak in all the English history and literature that you want. We can go to the University of London. They have our programs," he said.

We were driving home from Baltimore where we were looking for a dress that I could wear on the beach for our wedding. I realized having him with me was breaking all the traditions, but we were breaking them anyway, and I wanted him to help me find the right thing to wear. After all, I'd helped him with his outfit.

"We've probably missed the application deadline," I said.

"Yes, you may have, but I didn't," he confessed. "I thought about applying last year and sent my application off. I got in for fall. You could probably get in for spring," he said.

"You applied without telling me?" I asked, shocked.

He fidgeted and couldn't look me in the eye.

"I thought maybe if I got in I could convince you to take this adventure with me. We could start our life together somewhere far away, with little interference."

"That was a little backhanded, wasn't it? I mean, you could have just asked me about it, right?"

"I could have, but you may have said it's all about my career and future goals and I wasn't taking you into consideration."

"Well, are you?" I asked.

"You are my number one consideration," he said, and squeezed my hand.

* * *

When I walked in the door after Michael dropped me off, my father saw the packages in my hands, one from a boutique in Baltimore on Charles Street.

"So, what did you get?" he asked.

"A dress for the wedding."

I started to head up the stairs.

"Why don't you show me what you got?"

I paused, feeling like it was a trick question. My father rarely asked me what I bought on my shopping sprees. I took two steps down to meet his eyes.

"You want to see the dress?"

"Yes, of course," he said, as if it weren't the craziest request anyone would make.

"It's in here," I said, lifting up the tissue paper so he could get a look inside the packaging.

"No, sweetie. I want to see what it looks like on you. I want to see how you will look on your wedding day on the beach. I promise, I won't tell my future son-in-law."

There was something about this request that was strange. I didn't want to put it on right now. Luckily, my mother saved the day.

"I got the Manor House Inn booked for the reception party for the first weekend of August," she said. "We really should talk about the caterer and band ideas."

I nodded, tucked the packages under my arms, and headed upstairs to my room. It was still apple green with pink lace curtains and two purple peace signs on the wall, remnants of my teen years. I looked at myself in the white, wooden full-length mirror, and took out the dress. I didn't put it on, but I held it in front of me as I studied my reflection.

I had a hard time looking myself in the eyes.

* * *

Our parents went down to the Caribbean early. We had decided to marry on the beach in Nevis and then have a reception when we got back. I had won this fight, and despite my parents' desire for a large wedding, they caved. They had packed and departed, leaving us behind for a day.

Michael had been working post-graduation in Washington, D.C. at a television station writing news copy, and the earliest flight we could get was at four in the afternoon out of Baltimore. He insisted on packing and driving himself to the airport instead of having to come home in rush hour to pick me up and run the risk of missing our flight. I took a cab to the airport.

I arrived for our flight much too early. The marriage jitters were probably getting to me, and I started to feel lightheaded and experienced tightness in my chest. I'd never experienced a panic attack before, but I sensed it was happening to me. I tried to reassure myself that I would calm down once Michael arrived.

I sat at the gate fidgeting. I began to perspire and watched other people scurry about in the corridors. I observed two older people holding hands walking toward their gate; I watched a young mother help her two children with their luggage and bags; I saw single people come and go, and I witnessed an attractive, stylish couple, not much older than myself, have a very animated argument in front of a small crowd.

"You don't understand me," she was saying to him.

"Yes, I do," he said. "More than you know."

"Do you think I'm your slave? Cook and clean and pack your stupid luggage bag before we go anywhere? Admit it! You're the one who forgot the camera! Not me!"

He rolled his eyes at her and walked away. She planted herself in the open chair that faced the glass windows, crossed her arms and legs, and stared at the planes as they taxied by, rolling out to the runway about to depart into the skies.

I watched her sit by herself, but only for a few minutes, because he returned and sat next to her with a soda in hand and a copy of what might have been her favorite magazine in the other. With a quick kiss, it seemed all was forgiven.

But this situation, and the others that were unfolding around me, made me realize that I had not been single—ever—in my adult life. I was young and I had always been with Michael. Was I about to enter a matchmaker-styled marriage, Michael chosen for me by Remzi and Carol Contelli and my own, doting parents? I felt like I couldn't breathe.

And then it happened. It was almost as if my body were being controlled by someone else. My legs began to move at a very fast pace away from the gate, away from the windows and planes and arguments. In a split second, I knew that if Michael got to the airport and found me there, I wouldn't have the opportunity to change my mind, so I made the decision to leave. My heart was pounding, and my head was swimming with thoughts too overwhelming to dissect. However, the one clear thought I had was this: I knew that if I changed my mind before he got there, if I left, then I could be saved from a planned life, of a life where I would be intimate with only one man, where I had put all of my dreams into a boy who was five, swinging on my swing set and playing flashlight tag in the dark. A boy who pushed me around in a wheelbarrow and claimed that he loved me for fifteen years; a boy who said he always knew we were meant to be. Getting out of the airport was the only way, I convinced myself, for salvation. I loved Michael, that I knew, but was it enough to surrender the rest of my life to him? To subject us both to families who wanted to be involved in every aspect of our lives?

Deserting him at the airport that day was the horrible, unforgivable thing I did to Michael Contelli. It's one of the most awful and cowardly things anyone can do. When the cab driver dropped me off at the home of my parents, I knew I had to leave word for Michael that I was okay, but had a change of heart, and the only thing I could do was leave a message on his parents' answering machine, where I guessed he would eventually go when he realized I was not at the airport. On the answering machine, I simply said, "Michael, I'm so sorry, but I cannot do it. I hope you will forgive me. I'm so sorry."

I placed a call to my parents in Nevis, but only got the operator at the hotel; my parents were probably on the beach sipping Pina Coladas.

"Please, you must get a message to them," I said through tears to the nice woman on the other end of the line. "Please tell them there will be no wedding. Their daughter is not coming to Nevis," I said, making the operator repeat it back to me. I wasn't sure anyone would ever speak to me again—not Michael, my mother, my father, or the Contellis.

The last time I spoke to Michael had been earlier in the morning in his driveway.

"I can't wait to see you at the airport, Annabelle. I love you so much. I can't wait to start our life together," he had said before he left for work. He kissed me then, a long, passionate, sweet kiss, full of hope and promise for our future together.

I wrote a note, placed it in an envelope, and left it for him where I hoped he'd find it. I then threw the already-packed suitcase back into my car and headed to see the only person I thought could help me sort out my life: my grandmother, Viviana.

* * *

Viviana was always called Vivi and never wanted to be called

Grandma or Nanny or Nonna. Even as a child she insisted that I simply called her Vivi. She lived in a waterfront cottage in St. Michael's, about forty-five minutes away on the Eastern Shore. She'd moved there with my grandfather from New York two years after my parents relocated to Maryland. Vivi was a smart woman, not because she was highly educated and had owned a small public relations firm for years before retiring, but because as much as she loved her daughter, she knew a little bit of distance between them would be healthy, and so she chose not to live in Annapolis.

Her house was one of my favorite places to visit. After my grandfather died ten years ago, I would come for extended periods of time to keep her company. Vivi worked part-time as a town administrator, helping to organize functions and festivals, so I was able to help out with events she was planning. The folks in town nicknamed me "Shadow" because I would follow her around and help her with events and functions. On the weekends when she didn't have something to do and was feeling lonely, she would drive to Annapolis to assist my mother in her pastry shop.

Vivi had been invited to Nevis for the wedding, but she had broken her foot when she accidentally twisted it the wrong way as she descended a short flight of stairs and missed her step. She called me to let me know she'd rebooked her flight and was going to arrive just two days later than originally expected. We'd all been so busy, I didn't even have a moment to tell Michael about it. Therefore, he thought she was already in the Caribbean with our parents.

Vivi's laid-back style was one I admired; she knew when her input was needed and when to offer quiet support. She never pressured me and was always there for me. For that reason, I knew there was a place I could go where I'd be welcome, and someone who cared about me would open the door.

It had become dark on my drive over, and I hadn't called before I left the house to tell her what I'd done. I couldn't bear to tell her on the telephone. Quite honestly, I needed a hug. And a good cry.

I rang the doorbell and could hear the soft sounds of Perry Como coming from inside. She had seen him several times in concert and cherished an autographed copy of an old album of his. I saw the outline of her figure through the window as she slowly made her way to the door with a crutch. She moved the curtain to one side to see who was there.

"Hi, Vivi," I shouted. "It's me, Annabelle."

She opened the door, her big, green eyes wide with shock and surprise. Just seeing her and the confused look on her face made me start to choke back the tears.

"Oh, my goodness! Annabelle…what in the world has happened? Is everyone alright?"

"I couldn't do it, Vivi," I cried, hyperventilating, finally letting it all out, my words barely audible. "I couldn't marry Michael… I…I…"

"It's okay, sweetheart, come in. I'll make some tea. We can talk it through. Come and sit, breathe…" She put her arms around me, and walking in a lopsided way, ushered me over to the couch where she promptly handed over a box of tissues. Her cast was hard and there was a little rubber ball on the bottom so she could walk on it. She put the crutch near the door and hobbled her way to the kitchen.

"How is your foot?" I mumbled, sniffling and reaching for the tissues.

"It's nothing compared to your present condition!" she said. "We'll have a chat about it in a minute."

This was why I loved her. She was the best listener. She wouldn't force me to do or say anything that I was not prepared to do or say. She had the patience to sit and hear me out, dissect the information, and help me cope with what I'd done. I heard her put the teakettle on.

Her cat, Muffins, jumped into my lap and purred. She was used to me. When I was in high school, before Michael, I'd spend part of my summers here, three or four weeks at a time, sometimes more. Vivi helped me get a job at Scully's, a clothing store on the corner of Main Street that her friend Nanette owned. I helped out during the week when I'd stay and one day on the weekends. Muffins was only a kitten then and would sometimes sleep in my room. Her tail curled as I petted her soft, gray head. I saw a teardrop land on her fur, but she didn't seem to mind. Cats like Muffins were used to adversity and could fend for themselves. They were independent. They got a little bit of loving, just what they needed, and then they moved on, exploring their surroundings, chasing things they shouldn't. They were mysterious, and at times I wondered if people ever really knew their cats. Or did cats always harbor a bit of mystique?

"Tea's ready," Vivi shouted. I knew she couldn't carry it into the family room, so I made her sit down and took the two cups of tea and sugar cookies and brought them to the coffee table. I'd never visited and not been offered sugar cookies, her specialty. There were always plenty of them in the white lattice cookie jar. Vivi plopped down beside me and put her foot on the ottoman.

"Now," she said. "Let's talk. Are you able to talk about it? Do you want to tell me what happened?"

"Only if you promise not to tell me what a mistake I've made and how Mom and Dad are going to kill me for this."

"I promise. I won't say it…but can I think it?"

I laughed, and pushed the tea aside. "This isn't going to work," I said, pointing down to the teacup. "I need something stronger."

She pointed to the hunt board where she kept her little stash of liquor. She wasn't a big drinker, but always had something on hand for those who were. "Would a shot of Jack Daniels do?" she asked.

* * *

Vivi's house smelled of gingersnaps and fresh pinecones. Even in the early summer it smelled this way, despite the freesia she had outside her doorway and the large hydrangea bushes that outlined her front porch. Her home was comfortable and welcoming, and after my second small glass of Jack Daniels and Coke, I felt myself loosening up, the knot in my stomach less tight and painful than when I walked through the door.

I unburdened myself like a sinner in a confessional. I told her how I'd left the airport in a panic and took a cab home; that I'd called my parents and left word for them, but that I hadn't spoken to anyone yet; that I'd reacted without thinking it through and that Michael would have arrived at the airport looking for me, been shocked not to have found me waiting, worried sick, in complete disbelief as he tried to figure out what had happened. Only after he arrived home and listened to his message would he have heard the words I spoke—*I can't do it*." All the while, Vivi listened intently and rarely changed the expression on her face. I admired the way she thought; it was as if I could see her processing and comprehending every minute detail of what I told her. The way she listened to me and comforted me that night—let's just say, I was grateful that she was home, and not in Nevis like she could well have been, waiting for me to arrive.

When I was through with my story, Vivi remained silent, reflective. I waited for her to respond.

"Well, Miss," she said, "I think you'd best get to bed. There is nothing you can do about it now, and you need your rest."

"That's it?" I said, incredulously. "You have no advice to give?"

"Not tonight. We should both sleep on it."

"Oh, so this is how it works? I spill my guts and you just listen and offer no feedback? Who are you? Glinda, the good witch? I have to learn it for myself?"

"You know, Annabelle," she said, "that's a great analogy and I guess I'm flattered that you'd equate me with Glinda. But you're right. You do have to figure it out for yourself. This is your life, and it's your decision. You owe it to yourself to sleep on it. In fact, you owe it to yourself to mull it over until it feels right or until you come to peace with it. Only you can make the right or wrong choice. And unfortunately, you can't click your heels to find the answer."

If only I could, I thought.

* * *

Vivi didn't stop me from having a few drinks during my crisis, and when I woke up the next morning, I had a headache. The sun was shining brightly, the light streaming in through the windows where I had slept. The room was pleasant, white and light, an old antique chest of drawers and a silver plated mirror sat by the far wall, and sheer white curtains graced the two long windows in the room. I had left them open during the night, and now a strong breeze was blowing them back and forth as they skirted the wide-plank hardwood floors. Muffins pushed through the cracked door and inspected me lying in bed.

I could hear Vivi outside, probably obsessing over her meticulous garden and wishing her foot were not preventing her from doing her gardening. Her long, flat yard backed up to the water, where she had a little patio and a bench set up down by her dock. When Pop died, she had sold the boat, and so the dock sat empty for years. She never cared for boating too much because she'd never learned to swim. I always found this to be suspicious because she was one of nine children, and according to Vivi, they all enjoyed weekends in the summer at the Jersey shore. Yet she wouldn't even go out on the boat with a lifejacket, she was so petrified.

After Pop died, she had also hired a lawn-cutting service—two high school kids who had started their own little company—and I thought I could hear her talking through the windows with them.

When the mowing started, I made my way into the kitchen where she'd left a pot of coffee brewing on the counter. I wasn't normally a coffee drinker, but this morning, I craved one, probably because the smell had seeped down the hallway and hovered in a cloud over my bed. Vivi was sitting at her kitchen table with her leg propped up clipping coupons from the newspaper, her reading glasses around her neck.

"Good morning, sleepy," she said. "Do you have a little headache?" I noticed she left a bottle of aspirin on the table for me next to the newspapers.

"Little one," I said.

"Good for you," she said. "If you're going to feel like crap, you might as well feel like crap all the way around for a day. It will remind you that you hate feeling this way and life will become good and clear again."

"Such philosophy so early in the morning, Vivi," I said.

"Would you rather hear about how itchy my foot is inside this cast?"

* * *

After the landscapers finished mowing the grass and she had paid them extra to weed her beds, I made her recline in the chaise outside while I threw lunch together. I carried it out on a painted wooden tray, and then helped her over to the table where we sat under the yellow shade umbrella. There was sweet tea in the pitcher and petite sandwiches and a summer pasta salad on our plates. After her friends drove her to the hospital yesterday, they had organized a food run and had come over with four large bags of groceries for her. The spread looked delicious, and I realized I hadn't eaten since breakfast yesterday. Liquor on an empty stomach wasn't always a good idea.

"I've thought about what you did, Annabelle, and while I try my best not to meddle with you—or God forbid, your mother, who resents even the smallest suggestions—I do have a piece of advice. When Pop died, he said something to me that I'll never forget. We'd been married for forty years, and he was so sick with cancer, skinny, splotches all over his body, his skin discolored, the white of his eyes yellowed, I almost didn't recognize him physically, but when he spoke, I recognized all of his goodness. I sat there holding his hand, and I remembered I married him because he was the calming influence in my life. He was the touch of reality that never let me get too wildly crazy or too sadly depressed. Anyway, he lay in the hospital bed and said, 'This is it, Viv. You only get one of these lives. It was pretty good for me, and I hope it was for you too. But don't let time slip away. There's more ahead for you. Do what you want, what you love. And most importantly, love.' I think he was giving me his blessing to marry again if I were so inclined, but he was also reminding me about life and passion and to not let it slip away. It's funny, right? The things we take for granted."

It was quiet for a minute, and I thought about Pop's sentimental remarks, of how he cared for her, and how it must have been difficult for them both to say goodbye when his mind wasn't ready to go, but his body was through.

"You married Pop when you were young. How did you know it would work?"

"Does anyone really know for sure if it will work? We can think it will work, we can hope it will work, but ultimately both people have to want it to work," she said. "That's the key word here, Annabelle. It's never easy. It takes work."

"Do you think I've made a mistake and I need to fix it with Michael?"

"Only you can decide that," Vivi said. "I'm just telling you to think it through. You made a decision yesterday in haste or in a panic or whatever, but that decision will have consequences, not just for you and Michael, but also for all those involved. And unfortunately, as time wasn't on Pop's side, it may not be on yours right now, either."

"Can you be independent and be married? Can marriage and being your own person co-exist?" I asked her.

"Annabelle, honey, are you confusing things? You'll be married to Michael, not his family, and your mom and dad will back off."

"But did you ever feel any independence when you were married to Pop?"

"We always gave each other space, yet we always knew what was most important."

This was what my grandmother offered: gentle advice and a new perspective. I knew I could count on her because she tells it like it is, no matter how much it hurts or how painful it is to see my own flaws. She shuffled out of her chair to stand behind me. She hugged me, resting her chin on my head.

"We all make mistakes, Annabelle. I just want you to think it all through carefully. You owe it to yourself, and you owe it to Michael." She kissed the top of my head and made her way back to the chaise.

I ran my fingers through my long hair and pulled a ponytail holder out of my pocket. I put it up, as tight as I could stand it, hoping it would force blood to my brain and bring common sense into my thinking.

"You can't hide here forever," Vivi said. "At some point, you've got to face the music."

"I'm not in the mood for music today," I said.

Michael

Have you ever lost something—I mean really lost something—like your watch or your favorite sweatshirt or a child for a few moments? Have you ever looked for something you loved but couldn't find it amidst the chaos of your life? Moreover, have you ever thought you knew someone—I mean really knew someone—and then realized that the person you thought you knew only existed in your overextended mind and that maybe you imagined her to be someone that she wasn't?

When you get to the bottom of things, when they really start to unravel, they unravel quickly, like a ball of yarn or a political cover-up. You thought one thing, but it was actually another. It's the sucker punch and you're the sucker. You thought you were going to live your life with someone, and then you realize that the only remarkable thing about it was that you allowed yourself to become attached to a person who masqueraded as the love of your life. Imagine your surprise when you realized that she was a selfish person with no more respect for you than the fruit fly you killed earlier this morning as it circled surreptitiously around your desk.

* * *

I'd spent the day at work, trying to wrap up some loose ends, organizing the copy for some of the upcoming features for the week. It was my last day on the job; the station hired me temporarily knowing I was headed to England to pursue a master's degree at the University of London. After arguing about where we would live, Annabelle finally agreed to come with me. She was planning on applying for spring acceptance at the University, as well. I'd already been promised a job at The South London Press. My friend, Andrew, was in the process of helping us arrange a flat. He was already there, working at one of the hospitals, about to study medicine, eagerly awaiting our arrival.

"Andrew, I want it to be a nice flat. Don't put us in some seedy part of town."

"Trust me, I won't do that. I've got some places lined up for you to see. When do you two arrive?"

"One week from today," I told him earlier during a quick telephone conversation. "We're coming home from Nevis to pack our things and then we're off."

* * *

I'd left the office much later than planned. I was working on deadline and was stalled by a series of issues. When I got to the gate, frazzled and thinking I might be late, there was no sign of Annabelle. I checked my watch. I walked down the rows of seats. I didn't see her. I went to the check-in desk, but there was still no sign of Annabelle. I asked at the desk if she'd already checked in before me.

"No, sir," the woman said, her long nails searching through the list to see if Annabelle Marco's name had already been checked off.

"Are you sure?" I asked.

"I'll double check for you, sir," she said. After another minute, she looked at me. "I'm afraid she's not been checked off and has not presented her ticket."

Where was she? I thought. Had she been in an accident on her way to the airport? Did she forget something she had to go back for? Was she buying some magazines at the newsstand and just lost track of time?

I searched in my pocket for some change and ran back down the terminal to the pay phone. I dialed her parents' number, hoping she hadn't forgotten to leave. Our flight was due to depart in forty minutes. It rang and rang and rang. I looked around again, panicked. Something happened, I thought. Something is dreadfully wrong.

I mounted the escalator to the terminal and imagined her waiting for me at the gate, books and magazines in hand, excited about this adventure of a lifetime we were about to take together. We'd been over the wedding details. I pictured seeing the sparkle in her eyes, the smile beaming across her face, and her lips as they reached up to meet mine. I pictured handing her the bouquet of fresh flowers I bought from a vendor on the sidewalk outside the airport. We were about to become husband and wife. It should have been one of the happiest days of our lives.

Instead, I sat at the gate, waiting. Pacing. When our flight took off at four o'clock without either one of us on it, I sat in the terminal with flowers in hand wondering what I should do now. I needed to go and look for her. And I needed to start at home.

* * *

I felt nothing but dread. I drove like a maniac that night, swerving and passing cars, honking the horn when drivers were going too slowly, impatiently revving my engine at stoplights. I was acting like an ass, but I didn't know what to do until I got home. If she wasn't there—at either of our houses—I would have to call the police and ask about accidents. I wasn't prepared to make that phone call; I was petrified to make that phone call.

I finally made my way up the drive to Pendennis Mount and made the climb up our street. It was dark. I noticed her parents' house was dark, save for the front light they left on when they traveled. My home looked dark too.

I put the key into the door, hand trembling. Fear unnerved me. I immediately turned on all the lights and looked for notes. I ran to the answering machine, saw the green light blinking, and hit "play."

There it was.

"Michael, I'm so sorry, but I can't do it. I hope you can forgive me. I'm so sorry."

There was a click and then the sound of a dial tone. That was it.

I couldn't move. My body fell limp, and I staggered to reach the chair. What had she just said? What did she do?

Part of me knew I had to listen to it again to make sure I got it right, and the other part of me couldn't bear to hear her voice again.

How could she do it? What were her reasons?

I looked around the kitchen for another clue, a note, or some kind of message. I ran outside to the mailbox and opened it. Nothing there but today's mail. The kid my mother hired from across the street had failed to collect it. Then it dawned on me. Our spot. Something…she had to have left something…more detail…an explanation…a confession…

I ran out to the shed with a flashlight in my hand to guide the way, saw the blanket, the beer, the stash of notes, and then, there it was, a new one, right on top, with a small bulge in the envelope. I picked it up and felt its outline with my thumb and forefinger without opening it.

I knew what it was.

* * *

I had several strong gin and tonics at the Afterdeck, the letter jammed into my pocket. I stuck money in the pay phone outside and dialed the number I'd gotten from Information.

"Andie…have you heard from Annabelle? What the hell has she done?" I demanded when she picked up the phone.

"Michael? Is that you?"

"Who the hell do you think it is?" I yelled into the phone, practically choking on my words.

"Where are you? What's happened?"

"Your best friend skipped town, Andie. Skipped out on the wedding. Left me at the airport and you have no idea where the hell she is?" I could hear my own slurred speech.

"Honestly, I don't. Where are you? Are you alright?"

"I'm at the Afterdeck drinking myself into oblivion. How could she do it?"

"Stay right there. I'm coming to get you," she said.

Andie showed up minutes later, drove me back to my house, turned on all the lights, and put on a pot of coffee. I felt sick. I wasn't a big drinker, and I'd lost track of how many gin and tonics I'd had. I did a Tequila shot with the guy next to me who resembled an old sailor in a yellow raincoat. He let me talk, bought me a few drinks, and encouraged me to divulge more than I wanted. That shot was what probably sent me over the edge.

When I finally emerged from the bathroom, weakened and exhausted, I stumbled toward the kitchen table.

"Here," I said, digging the envelope out of my jeans as Andie handed me a cold towel for my head. "Here's what she left me."

Andie grabbed the unopened envelope and placed it on the table across from me. "No," I said. "Open it."

"I don't think now is a good time, Michael. You need to go to sleep. Sleep off all the crap you drank tonight."

"Read it, Andie. I can't bear to read it by myself. Please."

Andie opened the letter, and as she did, Annabelle's engagement ring landed on the table with a clink. I closed my eyes and put my head on the table. I could hear Andie clearing her throat, preparing to read it.

Dear Michael,

How can I explain how suffocated I feel? Quite honestly, I'm so confused, I don't know exactly what to say, but I do know that I've tried to talk to you about it and you've brushed me off. All along I felt like I couldn't talk to anyone because no one wanted to listen. Whether it was my parents, yours, or you—you all kept telling me it's all going to be okay. Maybe I'm not sure about it. Maybe I have an opinion. Does anyone really care what I think?

My heart hurts and I can't think anymore. I'm not sure what else to say except that I hope in time you'll understand.

--Annabelle

I got up from the table, crawled onto the couch, and tried to sleep off the nightmare.

* * *

I woke up in an uncomfortable position, the sun streaming into my eyes, which added to the throbbing head that already ailed me. When I turned and opened my eyes, I saw someone sleeping in the chair opposite me, her bare feet propped on the ottoman, a blanket covering her. I lifted my head the best I could and tried to focus my eyes—it was Andie, not Annabelle. Absolute confirmation: last night was a reality. It had happened, and had it not been for Andie, I may have tried to drive home in an intoxicated state.

It was ironic that it was Andie who rescued me—the very friend of Annabelle's I was never sure cared for me much at all. I stretched out, trying to untangle myself from the mass of blankets she must have thrown over me. My neck had a kink in it, probably from sleeping in one position on a rotten pillow. I moaned. Andie stirred, opened her eyes.

"You okay?" she asked.

"I have no idea," I said.

"I mean physically, not mentally."

"I have a wicked hangover, my neck is stiff, and I probably need a Coke and some Tylenol. Other than that, I'm fantastic."

"I was a little worried. I've never seen you like that, so I stayed."

"I don't know if I've ever been like that except for an episode at college when I went to some frat party and drank Tequila like it was Kool-Aid." I rubbed my head and groaned.

She stood up and started folding the blanket. I could tell she felt a little uneasy and probably didn't want to discuss Annabelle with me, which was fine, because I didn't want to talk about Annabelle with anyone.

"Your parents called after you passed out. I think they were surprised to hear a woman answering the phone at their house, but when I told them who it was, they were relieved. Just so you know, though, I was honest and told them what happened. I hope you're not upset."

"I'm a grown man, Andie. If I want to get piss drunk because my fiancee ditches me the day before our wedding, I'm allowed to do so. I'll call them when I get it together."

"Good, because they said they may be flying home today."

"So much for me hiding away from the world," I mumbled. "I'd get up and punch something if I could, but I feel too sick to stand."

"Sleep it off," Andie said. "I'll try to find her and…"

I interrupted. "If you find her, keep her. Don't send her my way."

She tilted her head the way someone does when they don't quite believe what you say. I meant every word. She just didn't know me well enough to know just how serious I was.

"Feel better," she said. "I hope it works out and don't forget your car's at the bar."

"Hey, Andie," I said. She turned to face me. "I appreciate what you did. Thanks."

"What are friends for?" she asked, and disappeared out the front door.

* * *

After several attempts to reach Andrew, a bag of ice clapped to my head, he finally answered.

"Aren't you supposed to be getting married somewhere?" he teased.

"Nope. Still single, my friend. No wedding. The bride was a no-show."

"You're kidding…"

"No."

"Where?"

"I don't know. Don't know where she is. I just know she didn't meet me at the airport and so I'm coming to London alone."

"When?"

"As soon as I can catch a flight and get the hell out of here," I said. "You still have some flats for me to look at when I get there?"

"Sure do. Just let me know and I'll arrange it with the agent."

"I'll call you when I know something."

That was it. I was a much more decisive than people thought. I was moving to London. Without Annabelle.

* * *

When my folks returned the next afternoon, my bags were already lined up next to the front door. They looked surprised to see them there. My mother's drama was way over the top that day. As if I hadn't endured enough, I now had to stomach her sympathy and condolences.

"Oh, honey, my poor honey. I'm so sorry you went through this alone!"

"It's fine, Mom. It's not the end of the world. I'll get over it."

Words were coming out of my mouth whether I meant them or not. I didn't sound like myself.

She hugged me and asked if she could make me something. I told her no, then my dad walked through the door with his luggage and parked it next to mine.

"Heading somewhere?"

"Yes," I said. "I'm catching a flight to London in a few hours.

I decided to go a few days earlier than expected. I hope you don't mind, but I just want to get as far away from here as I can."

"I understand, son," he said. "I just wish…"

I didn't want to get emotional with my father. We didn't have that kind of tenderness to our relationship, no matter how much we loved each other.

"It's okay, Dad," I said, "I don't really want to talk about it. I'm devastated enough. I don't understand it and can't rationalize it."

"She's been hiding out at Vivi's house," he said, quick to jump on Annabelle's behavior, which, I guess, we all had a right to do. "Her parents are furious. We're furious. She embarrassed our family."

"Not to get in an argument with you now, Dad, but it really has less to do with how it impacted you and mom. You guys have interfered with us enough. It's over now. No need to meddle anymore."

My mother was standing in the doorway, listening in as usual.

"I resent that comment," she said. "We didn't meddle in your life!"

"The hell you didn't! There was never any privacy at all. The four of you—you two and Mr. and Mrs. Marco—were like little old ladies sitting around gossiping. It's no wonder Annabelle couldn't take it. She felt smothered!"

"How do you know this?" my mother demanded.

"She told me. Many times. I just didn't listen."

"Well, what she did is unforgiveable," my mother piped in.

"Really? Unforgivable? You are making this more about you than me. This is ridiculous! Remember, she decided not to marry me, not you two!"

The house went silent. I'd never blown my stack at them before. I should have seen it more clearly. I should have forced

Annabelle to go away with me, away from the scrutiny and control they tried to impose on us. I looked at the two of them standing there, wearing expressions of indignation that I'd never seen—or noticed—before.

I knew then that I wouldn't be back for a very long time.

* * *

I was back at the airport thirty-six hours later. This time, however, I was flying out of Washington, D.C. Nevertheless, just waiting at a gate made me uncomfortable. I refused to allow my folks to come in and see me off. My outburst had caused tension, and I knew the sooner I left, the better it would be.

My mind was searching for all the clues Annabelle had left me about her uneasiness with marriage prior to yesterday's events and letters, but I kept coming up empty-handed. Had I not wanted to hear it? Had I blocked those conversations out of my mind? And yet I had stood there and defended her decision to my parents.

The airplane was buzzing, and we'd reached cruising altitude. I leaned my seat back and closed my eyes. I was convinced I was living in some kind of nightmare. I didn't feel like sorting through the rubble.

As recently as May, just before graduation, Annabelle had been lying in my bed in New York, the covers barely covering her breasts. I'd gotten up to use the bathroom and when I returned, she was flipping through one of my recent issues of *Sports Illustrated*.

"I need to learn more about baseball," she said. "I really like baseball. We should go to more games."

I sat in the chair opposite her, her face looking angelic in the morning, free of makeup, her hair tousled around her shoulders. I remember wanting to freeze that moment.

"If you'd go to grad school in London with me, we can watch cricket matches," I said.

"But it's not the same as American baseball," she said. "Don't they bowl in cricket, too?"

"Yes. It's bowling and batting. It's different than baseball."

She turned it over to look at the cover. It was the March 1987 issue with the three Ripkens on the cover.

"I wish I played a sport and didn't just cheer in high school. What sport could we play together?"

"Tennis. Golf. Softball. Bowling—"

"Bowling!" she howled. "Good grief! I was thinking of an outdoor sport!"

She threw the magazine across the room and seductively motioned for me to come to her with a curl of her finger.

"What?" I said.

"Actually, I do know an indoor sport I rather enjoy."

We spent the day in bed until, by two-thirty in the afternoon, when our stomachs growled so loudly for food, we climbed into our sweats and walked to a nearby diner. We ordered two Reubens, fries, and Cokes and sat in a booth near the window.

"It's good, this New York thing," she said. "I'm glad you went to school here. It's been fun getting to know this place."

"I'll miss it," I said, meaning every word of it.

It was difficult to believe that was the last day we spent in the city together.

Despite the man with the hacking cough who sat next to me and the teething, fussy baby who wouldn't let go of his mother's hair across the aisle, the flight to London was uneventful. The weather cooperated, and I landed early in the morning, a very red-faced Andrew there to greet me at the airport.

"Why is your face so flushed?" I asked him as he grabbed my bags and helped put them in a taxi.

"Sat outside all day yesterday at a football match. It was bloody awesome, but I didn't wear a hat. All red," he said pointing to his face.

"Are you already speaking the language?" I asked him.

"What do you mean?"

"Bloody awesome?" I said. "That's bloody British!"

"Bloody hell! It is, isn't it?"

The taxi took us to Andrew's place in Kensington where I'd be staying for the first few nights until I settled on a flat. We walked around the corner for fish and chips. I'd been craving it on the plane, and I hadn't eaten much since the debacle. I was famished.

It was exhausting trying not to think about Annabelle. It was difficult keeping my feelings to myself. I was worried that at some point I'd hit something or pick a fight with the wrong person because I'd never felt this kind of hurt and anger before.

Worse than that, it was painful to imagine that someday Annabelle—her smile, her light laugh, and her intelligent mind—was going to make someone else happy.

Annabelle

After two days, I drove home from Vivi's furious with myself. My hands were shaking and tears were streaming down my face. I couldn't see straight; I honestly should not have been behind the wheel of a car. My mother had called and chewed me out. Vivi had tried to protect me. I overheard her say to my mother, "Watch what you say…you're dealing with a very fragile girl right now," to which my mother said something along the lines of, "I don't give a damn, Mom! Put her on the phone!"

My grandmother handed me the phone, and my mother went on from there. I don't know if she took a breath in ten minutes. She subjected me to a ranting about how I'd disappointed them and how I'd hurt Carol and Remzi's feelings, my mother shouting that she hoped they would forgive her in time for my behavior.

But I wasn't crying on the ride home because of my mother. I was crying because I couldn't get the image of Michael discovering my absence at the airport out of my mind; I was crying because the person I trusted most in life was probably never going to forgive me; I was crying because Andie had tracked me down and told me how drunk Michael had gotten and how I didn't know a good thing when I had it.

And I was crying because I did know.

* * *

There was nothing worse than having to face the music and address the destruction that occurred, the direct result of your own actions. I wanted to crawl into a hole, but had to go home because it was the only place I had a bed; I had nowhere else to go.

I pulled into the driveway and saw no sign of my parents. I was hoping to sneak inside and crawl under the covers of my bed and die a slow death. My knees were knocking as I slipped my key into the door and made my way down the hallway like a thief in the middle of the night. As I turned to make my way up the stairs, I heard my mother's heels coming from the kitchen. It was too late.

"I am so disappointed with your behavior, Annabelle, I don't even know where to begin."

"Then don't," I said, turning to face her. I was not going to let her bully me.

"How could you do it? Why didn't you voice your concerns earlier?"

"Because I knew I had no one to talk to, Mom. Everyone would have told me that it was all going to be okay."

"And that's how you handled it?"

"Apparently."

"I don't like your attitude," she said. "Your father and I flew to the Caribbean to be a part of your wedding and this is what happens?"

"Yes," I said. "I'm terribly sorry it wasn't all neat and tidy for you, Mom."

I could see her face redden, her Italian temper working its way to a boil. "I don't know what you're talking about, but I won't let you paint me as your scapegoat. This was your decision and it's one you have to live with now. Do you have any idea where Michael is? Do you even care?"

I cared, but I wasn't going to let her know how much. I was going to fix it with Michael, without her help or the help of his parents. I shrugged my shoulders like an immature child.

"No," she continued, "you wouldn't know. He's gone, though. His parents took him to the airport earlier and he's on a plane headed for London without you. He told his parents he didn't want to hear your name, that he'd never forgive you, and that he'd completely misjudged you."

My face must have gone pale, because my mother knew she hit a nerve with those words.

"Better for him to move on with his life and you to move on with yours, seeing as how you don't want him in it," she finished. For all my mother's sweetness, she was a hardcore fighter, and she liked to come out on top of an argument, even if it meant hurting you to win.

"I will move on with mine, Mom," I said, the hurt and confusion of the last two days intersecting in such a way that my anger at her got the better of me. "And I'll start tomorrow by finding a job and my own place to live. I'll be out of here as soon as I can."

She was my mother, for crying out loud, but she was too worried about the perception and the feelings of Michael's parents. Did she not care how I felt? Did she not understand the confusion and panic I'd experienced at the airport? She never even asked me. I stormed up the stairs to my room, closed my door, and did what I wanted to do when I first got out of the car: I slipped beneath the covers and cried myself to sleep.

* * *

When I woke the next morning, I still had my clothes on and I hadn't brushed my teeth. I heard voices downstairs, and as it was a Monday morning, I thought—and prayed—they'd both be on their way to work. I tiptoed over to the door and opened it, straining to hear the voices at the bottom of the stairs.

"Why did she say she did it?"

"She didn't say."

"Didn't you ask her what happened? How did she come to change her mind?"

"I don't know."

"Well, she's your daughter, Donna. Don't you think at some point you should get to the bottom of it and ask her what the hell happened? How could she make such a snap decision?"

"Maybe it wasn't a snap decision," my mother said.

"What is that supposed to mean?"

"I don't know. I'm just saying maybe she has reasons why she didn't want to get married right now. Maybe she didn't think it would work out."

"Why? He's not good enough for Annabelle?"

"I didn't say that, Carol."

"What did you say, then?"

"I just mean, maybe something wasn't right. Who knows?"

"Well, I do," said Carol. "Something doesn't add up, and you're afraid to figure it out!" She was raising her voice at my mother.

"Maybe they couldn't deal with your constant meddling and fussing. Maybe Annabelle knew she'd never have a moment's peace!" my mother said.

"How dare you!"

Silence fell upon the room. My mother had crossed the line even though she was trying to protect me. She didn't like to be criticized. I knew she'd have the last word; she always does.

Nothing was said after that. The front door slammed, and I heard Carol's heavy footsteps outside. My mother huffed and walked back towards the kitchen.

* * *

The exchange I heard between my mother and Carol made me uneasy. It's disheartening to hear that sort of thing. It made me understand that Michael was gone and that I'd lost him. It was all starting to sink in and I felt ill. He'd left for England without me. This thought hurt me, even though I knew I had no right to be hurt by it. But it did hurt. Michael was off on our adventure, only now it was going to be his adventure. I wanted to kick myself. I should have gone with him, I thought. What we needed was to get away. What we needed was to start our life far away from here.

This wasn't the easiest thing to admit. After all, I had been the one resisting change. After I'd spent so much time in New York, should I have understood Michael's need to work and live in a big city? Maybe part of me was resentful that his career appeared to be more important than my own. I shouldn't have felt threatened by this, though, but for some reason, I think I was.

Did I not understand Michael as he understood me? Did I resent him for things that were out of our control? He was so intuitive and thoughtful. He would never have done this to me. I could tell sometimes how much he loved me just by the way he'd look at me, or how he'd open a door or pull out my chair. I could tell by the way he'd sit next to me on the couch and play with my hair, twisting it around his fingers, moving his hands around the nape of my neck. Michael was connected to me. Yet, did I ever allow myself to be fully connected to him?

I took a long, hot shower and then called Andie. In a week, she was moving to Baltimore to start a job in advertising. She'd been hired as a client services manager and was going to be working primarily on two accounts: a bank and a city hospital. Andie was the creative one in our group of friends—she'd headed up the art club in high school and in college was the president of the Ad Club. She'd been involved in numerous internships, and her most recent one was with an advertising agency in Baltimore she got through a friend in the business. The company loved her so much, they asked her to stay on full-time.

"Hi," she said sweetly. "How are you?"

"I can't breathe, Andie. I mean, seriously, I can't breathe. I have to move out of here. I have to get a job."

"What about grad school?" she asked.

"I still want to do it, but I can't live in this house. You don't understand."

"Yes, I do. I understand. Want to come help me pack and we can figure something out?"

"Yes," I said. "I'll be over in a few minutes."

"Have you talked to Michael?"

"No."

"Why not? I thought you were going to apologize and clear the air."

"It's not that easy," I told her.

"I don't understand. He probably wants to hear from you even though he's pissed."

"He may, but I'd guess not. He moved to London without me."

I heard Andie gasp. "I think you'd better get here right now so I can hear the rest of this story."

* * *

The first thing she said to me when I entered her home was, "You're face is puffy. Your eyes are swollen."

"You'd look this way, too, if you cried yourself to sleep and betrayed the man you love."

"Let's not have a pity party, Annabelle. You did the deed. Now you have to decide if you like what you've done. If you don't, there's an option: tell him you're sorry. Get down on your hands and knees and beg for forgiveness. On the other hand, if you can live with the decision, then move on. Tell yourself you had reasons to do what you did. Tell yourself you would not have acted that way had you not had some serious concerns about your life together. People usually make decisions based on gut instincts, right? Well, your gut told you to leave. You just didn't execute it in the most polite way."

I looked at Andie, her wild, dark hair curly, her skin pasty white. She was so wise right then, and I loved her for her support. She could be brutal at times with her frankness. However, I appreciated it then. She just wanted to help me come to terms with the insane decision I had made—or maybe it wasn't that insane at all. She was certainly right that if I hadn't given it proper consideration, I wouldn't have done it. Something did make me run.

Nevertheless, my mind was so jumbled with guilt and anxiety and fear that I just wanted to be in a place that didn't leave me feeling like the slime of the earth. So when she suggested that I come with her to Baltimore to the apartment complex where she'd signed a lease to check it out and ask the rental office if we could get a two-bedroom instead of a one-bedroom apartment, I said I would go with her.

Before I knew it, we were driving home trying to figure out if one small U-Haul would fit both of our belongings as well as the garage full of stuff her brother and his wife were going to pass along to Andie for our new place in Mount Washington.

"This is not what I thought would be happening to me," I said. "I am rearranging the course of my life, right here, as I drive home with you. I can't believe we're going to live together."

"I'm trying not to feel insulted by your tone."

"You know what I mean," I said. "It's just that four days ago I was going to be living in London as a married woman. Now, I'm moving to Mount Washington, without a job, with my best friend. My parents hate me, Michael hates me, his parents hate me, and on top of it all, I have to reapply to grad school. It's just insane."

"Well, when you put it that way, it seems that the brightest spot is that you're going to be spending a lot of time in a cool apartment with your best friend," Andie said.

She smiled at me and patted my leg. "You forgot one other thing."

"What?" I asked.

"You also need a job to pay your rent."

* * *

I taped up the last box and took the last few items from the rod in my closet.

"I can't believe you're moving out," my mother said to me, exhausted by my antics as I packed my luggage and boxed up my room.

"It's better for all of us, Mom," I said. "I'm a grown-up now and I need to get out on my own. Plus, I need to clear my head."

I was still feeling depressed and disappointed at Michael's departure. But I certainly couldn't fault him. He had every right to leave. I let him go, and though I was feeling some sense of independence, I was missing him. But more than that, I wanted to talk with him, apologize in person.

His parents didn't return my phone calls. I'd made two attempts to reach out and apologize to them in person, but neither one of them yielded a response. I also left a message on their machine asking if I could have Michael's forwarding number, but that request had also been denied with silence.

You made your bed, I thought. Now lie in it.

Andie showed up with the most beat up U-Haul I'd ever seen; it gave me pause and I wondered if we'd even reach our destination without it falling apart on the highway. It was a certainly a clunker. We spent the afternoon moving our boxes and furniture, her brother and two of his friends assisting us. It took us about an hour at my house and then two hours loading up everything Andie owned.

Right before I was ready to close the door tightly behind me, and walk away from my parents' house, the phone rang. My mother yelled for me to pick it up the extension.

"Hello?"

"I'm proud of you," Vivi said.

"Really? Why?"

"For being independent. For moving out and starting new. I think it's the best thing you can do for yourself."

"Thank you," I said.

"Did you ever get to speak to Michael?"

"No…his parents aren't exactly excited to call me back. I don't have his number in London."

"In time," she said, "things will get better. Time heals all wounds."

"I've heard that, though I'm still in shock over what I've done and not sure it was the right thing. But I guess if you had the strength to go on after Pop, I can muster up the strength to go on after Michael. After all, I was the one who ended it."

"Well, sure, honey. You're still feeling lots of emotions, so the right thing is to clear one's head and take a look at it from a new perspective."

"I just really need to talk to Michael," I said.

"I'm sure he'll be home at some point. Eventually you'll get in touch with him."

"Well, thanks Vivi. I've got people waiting for me outside. The truck's loaded, and we're ready to move."

"Best of luck, Annabelle. Call me when you have a new phone number."

"I will, Vivi. I love you."

"You, too, sweet girl," she said.

What I didn't tell my grandmother, or anyone else for that matter, including Andie, was that Michael had responded to me. I had snuck into the shed by the tree the morning after I'd returned home—the morning after I heard the fight between my mother and Carol, the same morning I went to Andie's when we concocted our plan to live together.

Michael's retort was sitting in the very spot where I'd left his. I guess he assumed at some point I'd be home, and since I couldn't break into his parents' home to search the desk drawer of the office, the other spot where we'd kept our keepsake letters, I knew that if he were to respond, there'd be something left for me in the shed.

It read as follows:

Annabelle—

It's been thirty-six hours since I waited for you at the airport. Those hours were endless. I was worried, waiting there like a fool, sitting and pacing in an airport terminal wondering what the hell could have happened to you. It is my right now to have a word, something I wasn't permitted at the airport or even in person afterwards. You have severed our relationship so callously that I'm in absolute shock. I sit here cursing myself for the trust and love I put into us for so long. You're kidding yourself if you don't think I know that part of your cowardice revolves around the nature of our parents and their friendship. I also know you resented our parents' involvement with us, and now, after reading your letter, know that apparently it was not only them who made you feel smothered, but me, as well. I can't believe you felt you couldn't talk to me about it—I mean really talk to me about it.

I'm sorry you felt that the only way you could change your mind was to leave and not look back. I hope you find this letter and know that I've left; I've gone on to continue our plans to go to London and pursue what I thought might be an adventure for us, a chance for us to start a life together away from the old one and the pressures that you felt.

I'm blown away by your ability to throw all the trust, respect, and love we had for each other out the window in one swift action. Or was it all pretend?

When you find this, you'll be standing near our spot. Remember it? Remember how we clicked? Did I mean nothing to you?

Five years ago, what we started under that tree had the potential to become something spectacular. You let it die.

I'm done playing the fool.

—Michael

That letter was the reason Michael and I never did speak. I moved to Baltimore and started a new life, and he moved to London and started a new life. Tensions continued between our families until they no longer talked at all. I know my parents blamed me for the loss of their best friends.

I didn't mean for it to turn out that way. When I left the airport, I never thought about repercussions. I never thought about the depth of regret and angst and hurt. I didn't take into consideration the long-term consequences of my actions.

The truth of the matter was, I loved Michael, yet my compulsive decision had altered the lives of us all, for better or for worse.

Part Three

Annabelle

It had become a tradition that a group of us got together on Thanksgiving night. Andie, Will, Linda, and I were among those who met in Annapolis at Charlie's. Charlie and Andie had been dating on and off for years, but they were back on again, and more serious than ever. I liked Charlie; he was down to earth, funny, and hard working. He'd owned the bar for about six years, and it suited his personality. Andie continued to live in Baltimore, but when I moved back to Annapolis, she mentioned on occasion that she'd considered a move back to the area as well. Part of me wondered if she was waiting for a formal commitment from Charlie before she made that decision.

I stopped back at my condo after gorging myself at my mother's family dinner. As usual, it was delicious, replete with a turkey stuffed with fruit that made it so tender and juicy, sweet potatoes, green beans, turnips, cranberry sauce, stuffing, fruit salad, and an amazing assortment of muffins and breads from the bakery. I had a piece of both my grandmother's apple pie and my cousin's pumpkin pie with whipped cream on top. My stomach was stuffed and bloated; I was having a hard time buttoning my black skirt. I washed my face, applied some makeup, put on my raspberry cashmere sweater, black tights, plaid scarf, and topped the outfit off with tall boots and a peacoat. I began the walk to Charlie's. I hated to drive when I could walk, and the city was quiet, with few visitors and only a small population of locals out on Thanksgiving. It had become so cold that I reached for the gloves I'd shoved in my coat pockets.

When I walked in the door I saw Charlie first. He was happily attending to his customers. He lived at his pub; he was always there schmoozing his clientele. Charlie was never quite clean-shaven, loved the outdoors, and owned a small powerboat. On his days away from the bar, he could be found fishing or boating on the Chesapeake Bay with friends. Wherever you found Charlie, there was usually an entourage of friends around him.

"Annabelle, you're here without your sidekick?"

"Andie's not here yet?" I asked him.

"No, but she'll be here soon. Her family ate an early meal, so she should get here any second. How was your Thanksgiving?"

"Good," I said, "but I'm looking forward to hanging out tonight with everyone."

"Will's here already," Charlie said, pointing over to the pool table in the back. He and Linda seemed like they were in a heated competition, so I positioned myself at the bar.

"What can I get you?" he asked.

"Glass of white wine, thanks." He told the bartender to give me a glass on the house.

There was a sizeable crowd inside, and I noticed Charlie had a special menu for Thanksgiving that included turkey, green beans, and mashed potatoes. Some of the folks were indulging, but I knew that not one additional bite of food was going into my mouth—or stomach.

Will saw me, gave a wave, and smiled. Linda peeked her head around the corner and waved too. My fingers were crossed; I hoped her jealous spell had faded. When they finished their game, they appeared beside me and hopped up on stools.

"Happy Thanksgiving, Annabelle," Will said, as he planted a kiss on my cheek.

"Thanks, Will. Happy Thanksgiving to you. And to you, too, Linda." I gave her a hug.

I was glad to see them, and we caught up on small talk. Linda was unusually chatty about her new job as the director of development at the local hospital, and Will seemed to be very proud of her, nodding along as she discussed her upcoming goals. Then Will and I talked about a piece he was writing for a national magazine. I loved hearing about his work. I was thankful he'd picked a date to speak to my feature writing class and share with the students some insights on freelance writing.

"So what do you want me to focus on? What are the students writing?"

"Profile articles," I said. "They are interviewing and writing this week."

The students usually got a kick out of him because he was blunt, honest, and funny. He shared with them the story of his career and how it took diligence and perseverance to write and become published.

"Your students seem interested in learning," he said, "so that must be a direct reflection on your teaching methods."

I turned to Linda, who was listening to every word we said. "I can see why you keep him around, Linda," I teased.

Out of the corner of my eye, the door opened, and Andie sauntered in. She grabbed Charlie, gave him a big kiss, and everyone in the bar started to hoot and holler. "Oh, shut your traps," she shouted, laughing.

I was so glad to see her. We hadn't lived together for five years, but I missed her spunky wit and her big smile in the mornings. She walked over and ordered herself a tall beer. Laughter ensued. Within minutes, more of our friends arrived, a mini-reunion of sorts, and we moved to a table that Charlie had reserved for us. After finishing a glass of wine, I excused myself to visit the ladies' room. It was then that I saw him.

He was sitting in the corner, at a table by himself. Our eyes met and locked. I felt my knees disappear, and I wondered for a second how I was still standing. He tipped his beer to me, I nodded, and skirted off to the bathroom.

I could feel myself start to hyperventilate. I stared at myself in the mirror, almost panting, forgetting entirely that I had to go to the bathroom. Oh, God, I thought, I'm not as calm as I thought I'd be. What will I say? What will he say? Of all the places in Annapolis, why is he here? And then I remembered: Andrew. Andrew was friends with Will and Linda. Maybe he was meeting them here and would end up joining our group.

My head was spinning, and I had a conference in the mirror with myself. Pull yourself together, I thought. You are thirty-two years old. This is ridiculous. You're not the same person you once were.

I started to laugh like a crazy person at my own juvenile behavior. I dabbed a little water on my face with a paper towel, trying not to mess up my makeup. I remembered I had to go to the bathroom and entered the stall. I took slow, deep breaths as I tried to calm myself down.

However, I knew I couldn't take cover for long. The few moments of hiding felt like an eternity, and I knew I had to face the ghost of my past. I straightened my skirt, tossed my hair, stood erect, and exited the bathroom. I looked immediately in the direction of his table. It was empty.

Andie was in the corner talking to Charlie, so I reclaimed the chair next to Will. "Did anyone come over to our table while I was in the bathroom?"

"No," he started, "well, yes. Andrew popped in, said he'd be back later, and he and one of his friends left to go to Mum's for a while. I guess they were meeting some other guys."

Will had obviously not deduced that the guy was Michael. I couldn't concentrate, and the turkey I had eaten earlier was churning in my stomach. Andie came back over and sat beside me.

"You know who was here, right?" she whispered.

"Yes," I said.

"I didn't say anything to him. I was in the pool room with Charlie and he didn't see me."

She watched me squirm, taking a keen interest in my obvious discomfort. "Stop staring at me," I said.

"Well, this ought to be interesting," she said, leaning back in her chair, crossing her arms, and continuing to size me up. I looked at her incredulously as she sat there giggling and smirking.

"I'm sick about it," I said. "I don't think I can do this tonight."

"It was years ago, Annabelle. He'll be back here in a little while, and the two of you can bury the hatchet."

I furrowed my brow at her as the knot in my stomach grew tighter.

"I can't stay," I said, standing and grabbing my coat. "I can't do it tonight."

She looked at me and recognized something I wasn't willing to admit. I once was a coward; that hadn't changed.

"You can't run away forever, you know."

"I know," I said, "but it's Thanksgiving and I don't want to do it tonight."

I kissed her on the cheek, made excuses to everyone, and left Charlie's, stepping into the cold air, once again alone and running.

Every other Saturday morning, I met with Delia, my therapist. I had made my first appointment more than two years ago after my mother was diagnosed with cancer. My friend at work, Vicki, had been seeing a therapist about her personal problems, and I was always somewhat jealous that she had someone who would listen and help talk her through things.

"You really should try it, Annabelle. I mean, honestly, she's the best dumping ground. You can talk to her about anything," Vicki said over lunch.

"Like what? Not that I'm trying to pry, but what do you discuss with her?"

"Mostly my crap marriage, and how I have to work forty hours a week and do everything with the kids while he thinks nothing of playing golf and going to football tailgates," Vicki said bitterly. "Just stuff like that. She helps me cope."

I liked that term "cope," and so I started going. I couldn't wait to unload some new stuff on her, especially because I had the dream again. And I genuinely admired my therapist's determination to be serious, something I thought she worked hard at because we were so close in age. I could also tell she tried to disguise a quick wit.

"So, this is the dream you have been having for about ten years now?" she asked me, scribbling notes on the paper.

I was reclining on her couch; I usually sat in the chair next to her, but I was tired and had a pounding headache. Ever since Thanksgiving night, my stomach had been in knots.

"Why did you just sound like Harry in 'When Harry Met Sally?'" I asked.

"I'm not familiar with it."

"What kind of a therapist does not know that movie? Come on! Harry and Sally are walking through Central Park with the leaves all around them and she tells him she has a recurring dream where a faceless guy rips off her clothes…she has this dream over and over except she varies what she's wearing. It's a riot! I don't know—you just reminded me of that movie when you asked me about my dream."

"Yes," she said, "in fact, can we get back to that?"

I adored this woman. When I was in a session with her, she hunkered down. She focused. She'd been a big help over the past couple of years; however, she was fascinated by this dream disclosure. I think she felt betrayed because I'd been having this dream for so long, and it was the first time I had mentioned it to her.

"Okay, in my dream, a tornado is coming. The wind is whipping and I'm panicked—panicked because I have to get my family and friends to safety in the basement. Once they are there, I stand at the door and see the funnel in the distance. It's coming toward me, and I'm fascinated by it. I stand there alone watching it. And then I wake up."

She was scribbling furiously on her yellow legal pad. Sometimes when she did that I wondered if she was listening or doodling "nut job" at the top of the page. I watched to see what she did. She scratched her chin, switched the position of her legs, twirled her blond ringlets, and adjusted her glasses. Her name was Delia, and her name suited her. She was proper and fashionable, with a hint of trendy thrown in for good measure.

"Anything else you want to tell me about this dream?"

I thought for a moment. "Yes. It's usually in black and white, just like in the 'Wizard of Oz.' Remember when Dorothy sees the tornado coming? It's sort of like that."

"Did 'The Wizard of Oz' disturb you as a child?" Oh God, I thought. She wanted to hear more about my mother, our relationship, and my childhood.

"My mother took me to see it in a movie theatre when I was five. It scared the living daylights out of me. But it wasn't the witch or the flying monkeys that scared me. It was the tornado."

"Have you ever experienced a tornado?"

"Never."

She reached for her book on dreams and asked me to close my eyes and think of what the tornado represented. She had several theories, but then she silently mulled over the dream, read more of the text, adjusted her glasses again, and then spoke softly.

"If I'm interpreting this correctly, the tornado—and the fact that you, in particular, in the end of the dream, stand there alone watching it—has something to do with your need for independence. You want to be in control of your own destiny, and while you are concerned about everyone else, it's you who pulls the strings."

I thought for a moment. I stared through the open mini blinds of the large window and watched a little bluebird that was perched on the outside flowerbox. It looked toward us and then flew off, perhaps in search of its rainbow. "Do you think I'm right, Annabelle?" she asked again pensively. Her glasses rested on the tip of her nose and her eyes peered over them.

I couldn't keep it in any longer. I knew I had to tell her about running into Michael. She asked how that made me feel. I told her I realized that my search for independence came at the expense of perhaps the most important relationship in the world to me. Because of our limited time, I told her as much as I could about our past, my mistake, and the remorse I'd lived with for years.

She mulled over my situation, offered me some advice on how to handle conflict, and basically instructed me to never run from confrontation again.

"You are not allowed to run from your troubles like one would run from a tornado," she said. "This time you have to meet it head on, and perhaps that's what your dream was telling you by the way you stared at the approaching tornado. You might finally be ready to confront it." After ten years, let's hope so, I thought.

I could tell by her body language that she felt like she made a breakthrough with me. She looked pleased that she made progress, but I couldn't leave her that satisfied.

"So why do I dream in black and white?" I asked her.

She pursed her lips, thought for a moment, and said, "For that, you'll have to ask Stephen Spielberg."

Good for her, I thought. She actually tried to make a little joke.

* * *

My mother called me Saturday evening. After I had left Delia's office, I spent a few hours at the school library grading papers and preparing for classes.

"What are you up to, Bella?" she asked me.

"Nothing except trying to decide where I'm going to put my Christmas tree."

"Oh, did you go and get one already?"

"No," I said. "I thought I was going with you and Dad."

"Yes, that's why I'm calling. Do you want to go in the morning to Homestead Gardens?"

"That would be great," I said. Homestead Gardens was one

of my favorite holiday places to visit in the area. The nursery was located in Davidsonville, west of Annapolis, and its large shop was filled with unique Christmas decorations, an indoor and outdoor tree display, and a train garden.

"I want a very large tree," my mother said. "The biggest one I can find. I want to put it by the windows this year now that I've rearranged the furniture."

"Sounds good," I said.

"Hey, Mom," I started to say, wanting to ask her if she'd seen Michael yet.

"Yes, sweetie?"

I chickened out, realizing that my running days were not quite behind me. "I'm looking forward to it, and thanks for Thanksgiving."

We hung up, and I made myself a cup of tea. My throat was beginning to feel scratchy, and I wondered if I were coming down with something. It was probably a good decision not to involve my mother in my own dilemma with Michael; we'd been through that before and it had taken years for our relationship to get back on track.

After I'd initially moved out and into the apartment with Andie, I got a job working for a small publisher in Baltimore copyediting textbooks. It didn't pay much, but the company was extremely understanding about the time I needed for graduate school. I ended up working every day until about three and took my graduate courses in the evening. I traveled to College Park, which was a good forty-five minute ride for me each way from my apartment. For a couple of years, I was so busy with school and work that I had little time for anything else. My mother checked on me occasionally, but it was Vivi who was my touchstone. She called me twice a week to see how I was and even came to visit Andie and me once a month, usually on a Sunday. We'd take her to a brunch place we liked in Mt. Washington Village, and she was always buying us groceries, Berger cookies, and plants for our apartment.

"You girls keep me young," she said when we'd tell her outrageous stories of college life and work. Sometimes we'd make Vivi laugh so hard, she would actually snort.

Over a year after the fiasco with Michael, Vivi urged me to visit my parents to straighten things out.

"Why do I have to apologize?" I asked her.

"You don't exactly have to apologize—I never said that. You just have to clear the air."

"Shouldn't they apologize for ostracizing me?"

Vivi paused, then said, "Who is going to be the bigger person here? I can't speak to your mother, and you have more sense." She made me laugh when she spoke this directly, especially when she tossed in a bit of frustration when addressing my mother's behavior.

Finally, Vivi's persistence paid off. I took her advice and went home one afternoon to clear the air.

I knocked on the door, my parents completely unaware that I was coming, and my father came to the door. He kissed me and seemed genuinely happy to see me.

"Your hair's gotten long," he said. "How are you?"

"Good, Dad. Is Mom home?"

We ended up sitting in the kitchen, and my mom made us hot chocolate. It was a very cold February day, the kind of day where it was so cold outside, your face ached from the freezing temperature. There was a fire going in the fireplace.

"I think it might be time for us to move on from what happened a year and a half ago," I said. "We haven't been the same since."

"You're right," my mother said. "We haven't been the same. So much has changed."

"I'm sorry for what I did, I really am, but after it happened, there was no way to fix it," I said.

My mother looked at my father and shook her head. "You could have gone to England to talk to him."

"Oh, Mom, that's a little ridiculous. He didn't want to speak to me. He wrote me a letter. He couldn't forgive me, so I didn't bother trying."

This was the first they'd heard of it as I told the story of the letter he left for me. All that time, I had kept it to myself. I hadn't even told Vivi.

"Well, that seems a little lazy, Annabelle. I mean, a personal apology is important."

I knew she was right, but I didn't want to continue arguing about the way I had handled my problems with Michael.

"I know, Mom, but I'm not here about that. What's done is done. I've moved on and I'm sure Michael has, too. I just want this to not be weird between us anymore. I talk to Vivi more than I talk to you two."

I was right, and they knew it. With a bit of effort on both of our parts, the relationship began to heal. The discussion had helped, thanks to Vivi's urging. Then, years later, when my mother became ill, whatever remaining animosity there was faded completely, and when she patched things up with Carol and Remzi, the world became right again.

My mother's illness was a wake-up call for her. She worked harder at her relationship with Vivi. We could all see the lines on Vivi's face deepen with concern as my mother battled her cancer.

Where once they were like oil and water, my mother made every attempt to put silly conflicts aside. Neither one of them ever told me what was said between them, but my mother relies on Vivi now, just as Vivi relies on my mother.

I was looking forward to picking out a tree with my parents. I'd decided to move back to the area particularly so I could be nearby when, and if, anything ever went wrong with my mother's health again. Because, in the end, we were family, and mistakes that we were sorry for just faded away after a while.

* * *

Cole's call came as I was getting ready to head to my folks to go to Homestead Gardens. It was only nine-thirty in the morning.

"Annabelle?"

"Yes."

"It's Cole. I just wanted to call and wish you a belated Happy Thanksgiving."

We hadn't had contact in four months, though Andie kept me apprised of Cole sightings in Baltimore. She had recently bumped into him getting coffee at The Daily Grind in Fell's Point.

"Oh, happy belated Thanksgiving to you."

"So how are you?"

"Fine, good. I'm fine," I stammered. It was awkward. "So, why are you calling, Cole?"

"What do you mean? I'm just calling to see how you are."

"And that's it," I said, more as a statement rather than a question.

"Yup. That's it."

"Well, thanks. I'm good."

"Do you ever miss me?" he asked. I knew there had to be more to this story. He must have been lonely or needed something. That was when I would get the calls the first time we split.

"No, Cole, I don't, as a matter of fact. You had two chances with me, and you sort of blew each one of them, don't you think?"

He didn't answer. Cole never liked to believe he was ever wrong about anything. He was far too busy placing the blame on others. His pampered upbringing from old Annapolis money fostered his entitled, selfish behavior. His noteworthy good looks— similar to those of a chiseled Chippendale dancer—got the attention of women. Instead of letting the silence get to me, I broke it.

"I left some things at the house and I was hoping to come by to get them. Is it okay if I come by sometime over Christmas break?"

"You can come get them now if you want. I'm sitting here in my boxers."

His approach was so vulgar; he repulsed me now.

"That's not what I forgot."

"Sure," he said, trying to disguise his inappropriateness. "Come by whenever you want. You still have a key?"

"Yes," I said. "How about if I get my things and then I'll leave you my key on the table."

"If that suits you, that's fine."

There was a pause and then he spoke again. "So, are you spending Christmas with your family then?" he asked.

"Yes, I'll be at mom's house."

"I heard through the grapevine that your old boyfriend is back in town," he said. There was no need to mention him by name; we both knew of whom Cole was speaking.

"I've heard he's back. Listen, Cole, I'd love to chat, but my mother's expecting me soon. I hope you have a very nice holiday and thanks for checking on me," I said, completely disingenuous.

"You too," he said, still unwilling to hang up. "Hey, Annabelle…"

"Yes?"

"I didn't appreciate you enough. I'm sorry. I should have made more of an effort with our relationship."

His charms had the capacity to sneak up on you, but I was through being fooled. I didn't believe anything he said anymore. He'd become a compulsive liar—anything for attention—and I knew deep down that his apology had nothing to do with me. Like everything with Cole and his own self-absorption, he needed positive stroking. When he was down, he seemed to thrive on my positive reinforcement to make him feel better about himself. I'd been through it before, and in the past, had understood my role. However, I wasn't going to indulge him again.

"Thanks, Cole. Gotta go," I said, firmly hanging up the phone.

* * *

On the drive over to my parents' house, I wasn't thinking about Cole, but rather about my brief encounter with Michael at Charlie's. I assumed he'd be spending Christmas at home with his family. The close proximity of our homes allowed for an easy peek over the fence to their yard and driveway. Sometimes I couldn't bear to look.

I'd begun to obsess about seeing him. I could feel tension in my shoulders and neck, and my heart beat a little more rapidly than it had in the past. Would he look at me with disgust? Would the first words we exchange be those of strangers? Would he be able to see in my face that I haven't been the same since it all happened?

When I arrived at my mother's house, my spirits lifted. She was nearly done decorating the house and it was incredibly festive; she had, once again, outdone herself. She had a decorator's eye, and was capable of experiencing the holidays as if she were still a very young child. Because it was only going to be just three of us Christmas morning plus Vivi, it was always a love of hers to make the holidays memorable and special for me, special for us all.

* * *

The house was beautifully lit, wreaths were hung from every window, the fireplace was decorated with fresh greens, red ribbons, and white candles, and the smell of cinnamon permeated the house. The only thing missing was the tree. And Santa. As a young child and believer in the man with the red suit, I was one of those kids who talked to Santa, presented a wish list, and walked away with a token, dreaming of what Santa had in store for me.

"All aboard!" my dad cried out and we all got in the car. Vivi had come for the day as well, a pleasant and welcome surprise. We drove to the farm in my father's SUV, my father at the wheel as I sat in the front next to him, and my mother and Vivi in the back seat recounting our delicious Thanksgiving meal.

"So, what are our plans for Christmas this year? Vivi's house or our house?" I asked.

"We'll be at our house for Christmas Eve. I've decided to have a little party." My mother, prior to becoming ill, was the queen of entertaining. Last minute or planned out, it never mattered; she knew how to make sure her guests left wanting more.

"Great. Who's on the list?" I asked.

"The whole Thanksgiving crew, some of the folks from Dad's

work and the bakery, the Jones family, and Carol and Remzi. There will be about twenty of us," my mother said.

I noticed she didn't mention Michael's name. It was very suspicious.

My pulse quickened, and that alone was unsettling. I could see my father fidgeting in his seat. He started to wiggle his thumbs, a clear sign that he was about to address something uncomfortable.

"Michael has been invited over as well, Annabelle. I feel like I'm about to lecture a 16-year-old daughter, but I want you to be on your best behavior. Your mother and I have just rekindled a friendship with two people we care about. This business between you and Michael needs to be left in the past, and you need to find a way to be cordial. I don't ask too much of you, but I will ask this," my father said, probably wishing he didn't have to address this at all.

He was right. I felt like I was back in high school and Dad was scolding me for being out too late, which was often the case back then. I was never fond of curfews, and my parents lived for them.

My mother cleared her throat, a sign that what was about to come next was something I didn't want to hear.

Silence enveloped the car, and suddenly I didn't feel like looking for a Christmas tree at all. My Christmas spirit had floated away, first thanks to Cole, and then thanks to the scolding. However, I understood my father's point about my history with Michael. Our story was old news. My father didn't ordinarily make pleas, especially not on his behalf. Normally a very private man with a terrific sense of humor, he was the least invasive of the four parents when Michael and I were together—he'd even held his tongue ten years ago when it was the worst time of my life.

I drew in a deep breath, determined to act with grace and maturity about the entire situation, to show that I'd changed, and then I spoke, slowly and promisingly.

"I will do my very best to greet Michael warmly, Dad."

He reached over and gave my hand a squeeze.

* * *

The tree we selected for my parents' house was tall and full—there wasn't a bald spot on it. A blue spruce, it was about twelve feet high and picture perfect. It would certainly fill the great room where she wanted it if she placed it dead center of the peaked ceilings and windows. My mother was obsessed with white, and the great room was almost all white -- white walls, sofas, tables, and accent pieces. My mother's talent for design would make it the most beautiful room for Christmas. Already the space had been interspersed with vibrant splashes of reds and sparkling silvers. The room looked like one you would see on the pages of *Country Living* or *House Beautiful*. The home oozed with charm and character. No doubt the tree would add the finishing touch.

I stood and watched all the children interact with Santa. I loved seeing their faces light up as they chatted with him about what they wanted for Christmas. As Santa made his way through the crowd, he saw me standing there.

"HO-HO-HO, young lady," he said to me. "What would you like for Christmas?"

He caught me off guard, but my own response stopped me in my own tracks. I heard myself saying it. "Peace with an old friend."

He patted my head and handed me a candy cane. "Santa will do his best," he said.

We watched the children for a few minutes as we sipped hot

chocolate. It was a very chilly, damp day. It felt like it could snow, but there was no sign of it in the forecast.

We tied the trees down on the roof: the monstrous one for Mom and Dad and the little one for my condo. We got back in the car and headed for home, as we listened to Christmas carols. I sat back and closed my eyes on the ride and pictured Delia in her office sitting in front of me in her red chair, her Ph.D. diploma hanging behind her, legs stretched out, notepad in her hand, as she removed her glasses and said to me, "It's all about forgiveness, Annabelle. But first you have to forgive yourself."

Easier said than done, I thought. Easier said than done.

* * *

When we arrived at the house, my mother headed straight for the kitchen to make us lunch and Vivi followed. It was another of our traditions to decorate the tree together. I decided to stay for the festivities, and my father had promised to help me get my tree over to my place afterwards. I watched my father through the front bay window as he struggled to get the tree off the top of the car. He was having difficulty, so I put my coat back on and headed down the long driveway.

During the short time it took me to grab my jacket and head out the door, someone else must have seen Dad struggling. As I approached, I realized it was Michael.

"Thanks a lot, Michael," my father said, not seeing me walking towards them. He extended his hand for a proper shake. "Good to have you home."

"Good to be home," Michael said, gripping my father's hand. "Let me help you bring it inside."

My father and Michael carried the tree up the driveway together where my father would mostly likely drill a hole in the bottom of the trunk before he put it in the stand. I knew I needed to offer assistance.

"Need help, Dad?" I asked.

"No, sweetheart, we've got it," he said, his back to me. Michael's gaze met mine as they rushed past me to the garage. They placed the tree down on the ground so that my father could saw off the bottom and get to his work. He thanked Michael for the help and insisted he could manage it from there. Michael began to head back down the driveway to where I was standing, just an earshot from the garage.

I couldn't take my eyes off him.

"Hello," he said.

"Hello."

I realized I was in a beat up coat and crummy boots, not looking at all how I imagined looking when we had our first encounter.

"Good to see you," he said.

"You too," I said. I sounded like a parrot.

He started to come closer, perhaps feeling uncomfortable that my father could most likely hear our conversation. We stood there, like two frozen statues, staring at each other without saying a word, expressionless. It was so tense it almost hurt. I decided to break the ice.

"So, welcome back. Are you glad to be home?"

"Yes, thanks. It's been a long time."

Ten years, I thought. Ten years.

I continued to initiate the conversation. "My mother tells me you may be coming over on Christmas Eve for a party."

"Actually, I hadn't decided yet," he said.

He kicked a stone across the driveway and I watched him closely. I had always found Michael to be very handsome—sexy—and he looked particularly good at present. His hair was a little longer than I remembered it, but still dark, absent of any gray. He looked fit, though it was tough to tell for sure. He was wearing jeans and a leather jacket, and his black shoes looked brand new. He had matured, but only in the most pleasant of ways. The eyes that once looked at me with care and love were still hazel, and he looked tan—that lovely olive skin of his still glowing, even in the month of December. But it was his smile I wanted to see—his perfect white teeth and that cheeky grin.

"I hope you can make it. I mean, just imagine the food!" I said teasing him.

It took a moment for him to respond. "I'll think about it," he said as he lifted his eyes to meet mine. There was still no smile.

"Good."

My mother shouted out to us that lunch was ready. I felt it was an appropriate time to exit.

"I'd better go, then," I said, still searching his face for a sign of something—anything. "I hope to see you on Christmas Eve."

He nodded and began to walk back towards his house. I couldn't let him go.

"Michael…" I shouted after him. He turned to face me. I took a couple of steps forward. "I'm sure everyone would love to see you," I said. I smiled at him.

He gave me a cautious wave and a half-smile back.

Michael

Bloody hell, I hated roller coasters. I mean, what was their point? I wasn't a thrill seeker and didn't like having the living daylights scared out of me. Up and down and round and round and upside down. I hated the feeling of not knowing if it was the beginning, middle, or end. This was why I'd sworn off relationships. They were the same way. Total rubbish. You went up and down and had to endure the highs and lows, and for what? Misery?

I hadn't expected to get emotional when I saw Annabelle. After all the time that's gone by, I should have been over it. I waited outside because I'd been home for over a week, and I had that morbid curiosity that kept brewing—that sick, twisted, warped sense that I wanted to see her. I kept telling myself I was over it. I needed to hear Janie's insight and wisdom. She would have set me straight. She would have told me to walk away. Janie had no tolerance for unbalanced women. She would probably have despised Annabelle simply for her past mistakes had I told her the unabridged version. But I never did. I never told her the whole story about Annabelle. I only told her bits and pieces. Even Andrew didn't know the scope of it. I never shared that kind of thing with anyone.

Janie would have helped me not to feel so screwed up inside. It was ludicrous, I told myself. For ten years I'd imagined how this scene would play out. It wasn't what I expected; she didn't say what I wanted to hear. And yet, I was walking back to my folks' house, angry like I was back then. She stood there so calmly, urging me to come to Christmas Eve, acting like we were two friends who'd lost touch and later reconnected. It may have been a crazy notion, but I still wanted to hear an apology—or even an explanation—even after all this time. But more than that, the fact that I allowed myself to be affected by what happened years ago made me question my sanity. It was nonsensical.

I wasn't sure I wanted to subject myself to Christmas Eve at their house and pretend all was well. It was a mistake coming here. I couldn't wait to get to New York. I prayed one of the jobs would come through for me. And fast.

I rushed inside the house and jumped into my sweats and running shoes. I didn't want to think about how she still got to me or how beautiful she looked standing there, pine needles stuck to her coat and dirt on her boots, her brown hair longer than I remembered, her skin still youthful, her eyes green in the daylight. I was heading out for a run; exercise had become my own version of therapy.

* * *

Two days later, I got on a train bound for New York. I'd calmed down since seeing Annabelle. So much for the peace I felt leaving London.

Last night, my mother made me laugh pretty hard, though. She was making her homemade pizza dough, a recipe that's been in our family since Nonni, my mother's great grandmother, first started making it over a hundred years ago. It was passed down through our family and used one boiled potato in the dough as its secret ingredient. The outcome was a Sicilian-styled pie, with thick, fluffy crust and sauce and cheese on top. I tried making it once in London, but I failed miserably at it and ended up throwing the heap of a mess into the bin. After a few glasses of wine yesterday, my mother threw the dough up in the air, trying to teach me again the proper way to stretch it and beat it to help it rise, and it landed on my father's head. I'd never seen my father laugh that hard before.

After an evening of complete indulgence in my mother's cooking, I was on Amtrak just like I used to do in the good old days. This train was like a second home to me then. For Annabelle too.

I made it to Penn Station with only a few minutes to spare. I stopped at a breakfast place and grabbed a bagel and a cup of coffee; I hadn't had time to eat anything in the morning before I left. I passed the vendor selling the honey-roasted nuts; the aroma emanating from the cart made me feel at home. I was among the moving crowds of people, the businessmen and the tourists melding into one. I loved the pigeons and sea of yellow cabs that were omnipresent in the streets, as well as the rush of people. There was a spirit and a pace to it. It was New York, the place for dreamers.

Dot Cranston's office was located on 6th Avenue, not too far from the station. I began my walk and wondered how the interview would go. I had sent a letter before I left London, and she'd written back that she wanted to set up an interview when I returned to the States. I promptly called her and we'd set this date. We chatted for about forty minutes on the telephone in what was a preliminary interview. The position was for a senior editor of nonfiction books, and I was excited about the opportunity to use my talents on different book projects.

When I checked in with the receptionist, it was only minutes before Dot's assistant greeted me and ushered me down a long hallway to a large corner office, windows ceiling to floor. I sat in an oversized leather chair, and Dot spun around to face me. She had the phone tucked under her chin as she wound down her conversation with the caller on the other end of the line. She was much smaller than I expected. She was a very petite, small-boned woman with severely pulled back white hair, her face more youthful than the shade suggested. She reached across the desk, and I stood to shake her extended hand as her assistant closed the door quietly behind us.

Her big, powerful voice was raspy and didn't match her look at all.

"Sit down, sit down. You're the one I've been waiting to interview. How was the trip?"

"Just fine, thank you. It's good to be back in New York," I said.

She searched her desk for my resume and realized it was on top of a pile right in front of her. She picked up her glasses and perused it.

"So, Mr. Contelli, why make the switch from newspapers to books?"

"I need a change. Not too severe a change, but a change nonetheless."

"You were at *The Times* for quite a while. Did you enjoy London?"

"Very much."

"How does it compare to New York?"

"It doesn't," I say, giving her what she wants.

"Are you back in America for good?"

"I believe I am," I said. This interview was full of quick back and forth comments, reminiscent of Ping Pong. She continued.

"Do you make your bed every morning, Mr. Contelli?"

"Every morning," I said.

"What is it about books that makes you want to work here?"

"Books have a sense of permanence that newspapers just don't offer, unless, of course, you're using the Microfiche machine searching for old articles. Newspaper articles come and go, but books stay around, have multiple re-printings, and have amazing shelf life. I like that. Plus, I like the way they smell. Far better than a newspaper." I leaned back and crossed my arms, happy with my response.

She smiled, made a few notes on her paper, and let silence envelope the room for several minutes.

"When can you start?" she asked, moving close to me and patting my back.

The abrupt offer caught me off-guard. It may have been an absurd reaction, but part of me wasn't prepared to hear those words.

* * *

Over lunch, Dot insisted that I could start after the holidays, which was a month away. I had time to figure out where I would live, which was never an easy thing to do. She showed me around, introduced me to folks, and admitted to having already checked my references at the paper. Janie and Albert apparently gave me quality recommendations.

"Rave reviews, Michael," Dot said in her cigarette voice, "rave reviews."

Since I was in the city for the day, Dot hooked me up with a leasing agent and made an appointment for later in the afternoon. It was strange how quickly it was all coming together; I guess I expected to go on many interviews before deciding on something, but the job sounded like something I'd enjoy doing, and I didn't want to turn it down. I needed an income.

The agent was a decent guy in his forties with a thick Long Island accent. He asked what I was looking for and what price range worked for me. We picked a date to meet the following week and he promised to line up several places for me to see. He asked me which area in the city interested me, and I told him "the area with the best apartment at the best price."

On the ride home, I was elated. Shocked, but elated. I wondered if my parents would be disappointed with this decision. I never asked them if they hoped I'd stay more local. But the publishing jobs I wanted were in New York—you had to be willing to relocate if you wanted those positions. Luckily, I would be close enough that a quick ride on the train would have me home in three hours. It would be a tad more convenient than being across an ocean.

As the train pulled away, I watched the city as it became smaller and smaller as we headed back to Baltimore. Over eight million people lived there, and I was going to be one of them. Annabelle may have caught me off guard, but I was determined to have solid footing. Perhaps I expected too much from her yesterday. Perhaps I always did.

I could never control her, but I had never wanted to, either. When we were together, I always respected her as her own person, supported her dreams, and was awed by her smarts and her comedic moments.

We passed Philadelphia, another great American city. I decided to go there for a weekend; I hadn't been to Independence Hall in many years, and although I'd been living away from here, I relished history and the stories of our Founding Fathers. Annabelle loved it too. We spent weekends in Philadelphia many moons ago, the two of us touring around, enjoying a waterfront blues festival, visiting some of the historic sites and buying prints at the Norman Rockwell Museum.

I wondered how she felt about it all now; I wondered if she remembered those days.

I wondered if I'd ever be able to let it all go.

Annabelle

I was in the midst of exams, grading hordes of them in my office, when there was a tap at the door. Vicky stood before me, her briefcase flung over her shoulder, her coat halfway off, sporting a mischievous grin on her face.

"You might want to stop by the main office," she said.

"Am I in trouble?"

"Well, I don't know yet, but it could be trouble." She winked.

"What are you talking about Vicky?" I was worried it was something related to work.

"Just go and see. You might want it."

I locked my office door behind me and headed to the building next door where the main office was located. The receptionists looked at me and together said, "What took you so long?"

"Did you call me?"

"Yes," the one woman said, "we left you a message."

"Oh, I'm sorry—I didn't check it. I just finished giving an exam."

The taller one, Gladys, picked up the very large Christmas arrangement and handed it over to me. "This is for you."

I stared at it. Red roses, baby's breath, white carnations, a little holly; the arrangement was thoroughly festive. I'd never had flowers delivered to me at work—ever—and certainly never from Cole. "Are you sure you have the right person?" I asked.

"It says your name right there on the envelope."

"Well, thanks, I guess."

I could tell they wanted me to reveal the admirer's name, but I tried to share as little as possible with colleagues. No need for the world to know your business.

I made my way back to my office, balanced the arrangement on one knee as I unlocked the door, and placed the flowers on the only clear space I had on a desk piled high with paperwork. I shut the door and read the card in private.

Annabelle,
May your days be merry and bright, and may no tornadoes be in sight.
—Delia

It was comforting to know I spent my hard-earned money on the right therapist.

* * *

Andie invited all of us to Charlie's for some Christmas cheer on Friday night. I was almost done grading exams and calculating percentages. Grades had to be turned in to the Registrar's office by Monday at ten in the morning. After that, my official winter break would begin, and I didn't have to report back to school until late January. I was looking forward to some time off—I had a stack of novels collecting dust on my bedside table. During the winter and summer breaks, I'd catch up on reading I'd missed during the semesters. Whether I was snuggled up under a chenille blanket with the fireplace ablaze or parked at the pool on a lounge chair, I enjoyed the escapism of quality literature.

I was ten minutes later than I wanted to be; I stopped at the mall and purchased a couple of gifts for fellow faculty members before I got home. I hoped Vicky would be pleased with the velvet scarf I'd purchased for her, and Bill, my other colleague whose office was adjacent to mine, was getting a set of 1950s classic music CDs. He talked all the time about how he used to be in a Doo-wop group, so I figured I'd let him enjoy the music of his day. We would exchange gifts at our traditional holiday party at noon on Monday, so I needed to shop and wrap before then. I also had to make a dish over the weekend to share, as well as bake Christmas cookies for a cookie swap. My colleagues shared a great sense of camaraderie, so celebrating in this manner was fitting; however, I hadn't finished my Christmas shopping. I left the mall and headed for Charlie's.

When I arrived, Andie was propped up on a barstool and she motioned for me to hurry up and come forward. I gathered around along with everyone else, not sure what the commotion was all about, and then Andie said out loud to all of us, "I'm so glad you're all here! I wanted you all to be the first to know!" She held up her left hand and a very large, sparkly diamond caught our eyes. She was ecstatic, and Charlie kissed her and congratulations ensued. While I was certainly happy for her, and not too terribly surprised because I knew how Charlie adored her, I felt a little left out that I had been told along with everyone else, and that she hadn't told me privately beforehand.

"When did this happen?" I asked her when we had a minute alone. "I'm so happy for you!"

"Last night. He let the assistant manager run the bar, and he and I went out to a nice dinner at Victor's Café. It was so great; we were at a table on the water and after we ordered the main course, he knelt beside me and said, 'I couldn't wait until Christmas, Andie. I love you. Will you marry me?' I was stunned! So amazing!"

"The ring is gorgeous," I said. "Why didn't you call me?"

"Honestly?"

"Yes, honestly! You know I would want to be one of the first to know!"

"I guess I was worried," she said. "I just wasn't sure with the Cole thing and now Michael being home…"

I saved her the pain of saying it.

"Don't worry, Andie. I can be happy for someone else."

I hugged her and was genuinely pleased for them both. I knew they'd be happy together. They had so much in common, especially their love of people and parties and friends. Being able to smile every minute and entertain with ease was a talent not many have, especially when it was required twenty-four hours a day. Charlie had that type of personality, and Andie did, as well. She was the glue that kept our group of girlfriends together.

Andie turned to face me. "Thanks for your support and love. I'm sorry I didn't call you last night. I should have known you would be happy for me."

Charlie offered us all glasses of champagne and we raised them in a toast that was given by Charlie's friend, Matt.

"Raise your glass, please, to Charlie and Andie. May their lives be happy and may the party never end," he said. We raised our glasses, "Hear, Hear," we said, and the music started to play while the champagne was poured.

I stood by myself, Andie and Charlie across from me with their arms around each other, laughing and happy. I looked at them. Did I ever feel that way when I was engaged? Did I ever feel that euphoria and wear that glow? I was so young, I could hardly remember how it felt; our engagement hadn't lasted very long, only about three months. But when I looked at Michael then, was it with the same sparkle that emanated from Andie's eyes? I certainly never felt that way about Cole, though I know I did love him at some point, before the lies, lack of money, and his habitual state of drunkenness towards the end. How was it we were able to ignore the negative aspects of people when we were in a relationship? We were only able to see what we wanted to see. When I was in love, I saw only the good things, never the bad. And if there were negative things, I ignored them, labeled them irrelevant or unimportant, made excuses, and forgave the faults before they became colossal. With Cole, near the end, I kept asking myself how I could have loved this person. What drew me to him initially? How could I have been so vulnerable? So blind?

When I was in junior high and high school, I spent a lot of time at my mother's bakery. My mother's taste in decorating boded well for her pastry shop because she replicated the feel of Confezioni Scandaloso—Scandalous Confections—an Italian pasticceria she loved in Siena, Italy. It was her favorite, and the one she visited time and time again when she traveled there with Vivi in her younger days, and then later with my father. Similar to Confezioni Scandalos, my mother's place was rich looking; it boasted cabinets and counters made of maple wood with marble countertops and trendy lighting around the bar area. She had scenic images on the walls depicting stunning Tuscan landscapes that one of her photographer friends took while shooting in Italy. To give them an old-world feel, my mother had them printed as sepia tones. There was a richness and warmth to La Pancia Affamata.

When my mother was very ill and could no longer manage the daily operation of it, I worked in her shop during the summer when I was on break. I spent long hours helping my mother's staff get her recipes just right. We made homemade Biscotti and Amaretti cookies, two recipes that had been handed down from cousins who lived in Italy. We made them fresh the night before. That experience was so stressful, not only because my mother was ill and could not physically come to work, but also because I was not a pastry chef like she was, no matter how many times we'd make her specialties together. Many of the recipes came out lumpy, but her patrons knew of her situation, and forgave my lack of baking prowess.

One night, I was staying late, and Cole showed up. I had sent everyone else home after having cleaned the place, and was attempting to make her Torta Caprese alone—her signature Chocolate Almond Torte—when Cole rapped on the glass door. I let him in and he began to help me, gathering the ingredients, reading the recipe aloud, rolling up his sleeves, and donning an apron. His capricious behavior was welcomed then, and we attempted the Torte together, the Italian music my mother loved playing softly in the background. I was so moved by his kindness that night, his thoughtfulness to be there for me when I was feeling low and worried about my mother's health, that we became intimate right there in her shop. We made love on the floor in the back behind the counter by candlelight on an old wool blanket, our bodies smelling of chocolate and powdered sugar. I cried about my mother. He told me he loved me, that he would never leave, that he'd never go anywhere. My mother became violently ill and was hospitalized the following week. I found out about Caroline the next day.

And yet, somehow, I took him back, despite his infidelity with a woman he met at work. It was remarkable what a skilled liar he could be. A salesman by trade, he knew how to work every angle—and people. It's a rare talent to be able to consistently beguile vulnerable women and feel no sense of remorse. But I didn't see it because I didn't want to see it. I was scared—petrified I'd lose my mother. Every self-help book in the world tells you things won't change unless you want them to change. It's like someone who smokes: the smoker can't quit unless the smoker wants to quit. All the people in the world, including those who love him most dearly, can't convince him to quit. He's got to want it for himself. The same was true with relationships: you had to see the flaws and want to see the flaws before you were able to decide what was best.

Delia offered insights into Cole's offenses. With her clever prodding techniques, Delia was able to help me see Cole for what he was: a lying, selfish conniver. After he lost his second job and we were living together, he became happily unemployed, perfectly content to allow me to go out and earn the money for us both to live on while he enjoyed himself. I had to cover the expenses on our apartment in Baltimore. It was convenient for him to live with me, though I was certain his feelings were not what they were. Nor were mine. After a while, I tired of the whole arrangement and his lack of drive. When my mother recovered, I knew I needed to get out. I talked to Delia about it.

"Then what should you do, Annabelle?" she asked. That afternoon, I called my former colleague about the condo in Annapolis.

I looked around at all my friends as we celebrated the engagement. It was a precious moment; it was sentimental and sweet. It was something to be treasured, I thought. It wasn't often that so much joy infected an entire room of people. Will sat down next to me and slapped my thigh.

"Did you know?" he asked.

"No, I didn't," I said. "It's so great for them."

"I guess the pressure's on now. Linda will never leave me alone."

I smiled at him and thought how lucky he was to have someone in his life who loved him.

* * *

On Thursday, the day before Christmas Eve, I had my last meeting of the year. My normally scheduled Saturday appointment had been moved because of the holidays. I was walking down the street, and snow was lightly falling around me. The weather reports were not calling for any accumulation, but the mere presence of flurries thrilled me as if I were a small child. I had shopped along Main Street, purchased a few last-minute presents, and picked up the one in my hand from the framer, neatly wrapped for my eleven-thirty with Delia. Her office was in an old brick building in East-port, just over the bridge that connected Eastport to the Annapolis Harbor. There was a walkway over the bridge, and I was scurrying to make the meeting on time. I was her last scheduled appointment of the day, as well as her last one until after the holidays. She was pleased to see me when I entered.

"If this weather doesn't put you in the Christmas spirit, I don't know what will!" she proclaimed, giddier than I'd ever seen her.

"This is for you," I said, as I gave her a little hug. She had become more to me than a therapist.

She opened the package. I'd written her a poem in rhyme—she didn't appreciate contemporary poetry—and even though I was not a stellar poet, I wanted her to have something heartfelt. She had helped me through many difficulties over the past couple of years. I was grateful to her. I could see she was touched by my sentimental gesture, and she read it aloud:

For Delia—
Create a sensation by feeling your way
Through moments of clouds and feelings of gray
Place all your doubt
In holes open wide
It glides through the air then
It falls; say goodbye.
Depart from yourself
Leaving tears of distress
And never look back,
It hurts even less.
—Your support has meant a lot to me. Thanks for making it all hurt less.
Love, Annabelle

"This is so beautiful and so touching, Annabelle." She sounded like she might cry.

"Don't get overly emotional on me, Delia," I teased. "You're the glue that helps keep it all together!"

"I know, I know," she said.

"I saw Michael," I said, changing the subject.

"And?" She was dabbing her eyes with a tissue.

"Nothing much happened. We just said 'hello' and I encouraged him to come over on Christmas Eve to my mother's party."

"Is he coming?"

"He said 'maybe.'"

"Well, maybe if he comes, it will be your chance to blow the tornado out of your mind. Clear the air with him; let him hear you say the things you've said to me."

"After all this time?"

"What? You don't think ten years is long enough?"

We assumed our standard positions for the rest of the therapy session, however, this time I was dippy with nervous anticipation of what the holidays might bring.

Michael

My parents were getting used to the idea of me working in New York—and living there again. I had placated my mother simply because New York wasn't situated across an ocean and because she knew she'd be able to see more Broadway shows. Ever since I was little, she was a volunteer with the local theatre in town. The company would produce three shows a year, and my mother helped with the business side of the production. My mother was a taskmaster, so her skills as a manager were a huge benefit to this small but well-respected organization. She probably always wanted to be an actress, although she would never publicly admit to it.

I was back from the supermarket; I had to pick up sugar so my mother could remake the lemon meringue pie she had destroyed. When she had attempted it earlier in the day, she realized she used salt instead of sugar when mixing her ingredients; it was a good thing she licked her finger when she finished mixing it up, or she never would have known. Imagine the looks on the faces of guests when they took a bite of that fiasco of a dessert at the big Christmas Eve dinner. After much deliberation, I decided I would go, though I still had reservations. However, I knew at some point all this nonsense had to be left in the past.

I grabbed the mail on my way in and opened a Christmas card from Janie. There was a scene from Dickens' "A Christmas Carol" on the front: Ebenezer Scrooge was opening his front door and was staring at the ghostly image of Marley on his doorknocker. Printed on the inside were two words: Bah! Humbug!

I read what she'd written in cursive:

Dear Michael,

Well, it's certainly not the same without you here. Billy misses your wry sense of humor and I miss you desperately at work—and outside of work. Albert is frantically trying to fill your position, but as you know, you're irreplaceable. I must confess to despising this decision of yours, no matter how I seemed to support it. I suppose I am just going to have to jaunt off to America to see you if I want to hear a dirty joke or experience the most wicked laugh I've ever heard. Of course, I could come cook you dinner...

Hope the family is well and you are settling in and finding a job that makes you happy, though you'll be hard pressed to find another colleague as intelligent and as cute as your former one.

Write soon with your news!

Miss you and Happy Christmas!

Love, Janie (and Billy, of course)

Billy would always have his hands full with that one, I thought. I read it over three times and chuckled to myself. It was ironic, though. I didn't miss being in London and doing the things I had been doing nearly as much as I'd expected.

"Thanks for the sugar, Michael," my mother said, as she started all over again from square one with the pie.

"Annabelle called for you."

I looked at her as if she had two heads. "Annabelle?"

"Yes."

"What did she want?"

"She wanted to see if she could stop by and speak with you, and I told her you were out."

I put the mail where my mother liked it, on the corner stacker near her little kitchen desk, and hung my coat on the peg rack in the hallway.

"Also, your real estate agent called and said that perfect place you wanted to look at in the West Village is available, the one on MacDougal Street. Anyway, he wanted to see if you could come up sometime after the 26th to look at it again and sign the paperwork. I left his number by the phone."

I called him immediately, not wanting the place to slip away from me. I asked him if he could put a hold on it. I had liked it immediately when I looked at it. It was a tiny one-bedroom with a den, a revamped kitchen with new appliances, large windows, and an updated bathroom in a corner building with great access to the subway. He said he'd try to secure it, and we hung up. I withheld my excitement, but if he could make it happen, I'd be thrilled.

My father was watching "The Bishop's Wife" with Cary Grant, so I parked myself next to him on the couch in the family room. We could hear my mother singing along with the Barbra Streisand Christmas CD she had on in the kitchen. My father raised the volume on the television.

"When she sings like that, I can't hear a word they say," he said.

We sat there for a few minutes in silence. I hadn't seen this film in years. I was reminded of how much I loved the old classics and how I respected them because of my parents. Besides, it was impossible not to like Cary Grant. The ladies loved him, but he was a guy's guy, too—he was suave, debonair, talented, and had great comedic timing.

"So, you're coming tonight, right?"

"I may not come over right away, but I'll stop by for a bit," I said.

"It'll be nice for us all to be together again," my father said.

I understood what he was saying. He was remembering the Christmas Eves of an era past, when our families and extended families got together. The year before Annabelle left me was the best Christmas I'd ever had. We were at our house that year. My mother was slaving away in the kitchen with Donna, music filled the air, snow was actually on the ground, and games were being played. Annabelle and I were happy. I knew then I wanted to spend my life with her.

She had given me a scrapbook for Christmas. It contained photos of us, letters we'd written back and forth to each other in college, remembrances from high school, our prom pictures, certificates from our activities, and photos of our families. I was touched by the effort she'd put into it, and we sat looking through it and shared it with everyone there. I often wondered what happened to it. I hadn't seen it in so long because when I left for London, I took very little with me. I could only pack the handful of items I could shove in my bag.

When the movie was over, I saw my dad was sleeping—and snoring—so I checked on my mother.

"Let me clean up for you," I said. "You've been in here all day. Go shower, relax, and get ready for the party." I grabbed the dishtowel out of her hand and sent her on her way to get herself together.

The pie was baking in the oven. The aroma that filled the house yielded a sense of warmth and home. In some ways, being away from home for so long made me wonder if I'd missed out on things, and I could tell by my parents' attention that I had been missed.

Annabelle

When the doorbell rang, I was upstairs touching up my make-up. Vivi had arrived, our first guest of the night. I heard the commotion begin.

"Put the music on, dear," my mother shouted to my father. "And make sure the candles are lit."

Admittedly, I was nervous; I had butterflies all day. My hand even shook slightly when I dialed the phone. Delia coached me yesterday during my session, but ultimately, she just wanted me to relax and let whatever I had to say come from my heart. I was sure that over the years Michael had probably questioned if I even had one.

In a simple black dress, tights, and tall boots, my dark hair curled for the occasion, I headed downstairs. When I reached the bottom, I heard the doorbell chime and opened the door for Carol. While our relationship still felt a little awkward, it was far better than it had been even a year ago.

"So good to see you," I said to her. "Here, let me carry that for you."

I walked her into the kitchen where my family was standing and placed her picture perfect lemon meringue pie on the counter. It looked like it should have been on the cover of *Southern Living* magazine. I was pleased to see she made it for us; it was one of her specialties.

"Where's Mr. Contelli?" I asked.

"Remzi," she said, correcting me, "will be over in a few minutes. He was trying to wrap some presents—last minute, of course! Poor dear. He's not very good at wrapping." She winked at my mother, and they exchanged knowing glances.

"Michael's coming, right?" I asked her, not really caring who was listening, but wanting to make sure he'd be there.

"I think he's planning to stop by," she said. My heart sunk. I hoped he wouldn't stay away. Not tonight.

The doorbell continued to toll, and soon, the room was filled with friends, colleagues, and our cousins. Vivi pulled me aside.

"You okay?" she asked. "Your spirit has deflated since Carol walked in the door."

"I don't know," I said.

"If it's about Michael, go knock on his door. Tell him to come."

I looked at her for more encouragement. She wanted me to take a leap of faith. She knew it was eating me alive—had been eating me alive—and haunting me for countless days and nights over the years.

"Should I? I mean, what if he just wants me to stay out of his life. What if it's too late to make an apology?"

"Maybe it's too late, but maybe it's not. If you have something to say to him, more than likely, this is going to be your best opportunity to say it."

She put her arm around me and walked me to the coat closet in the front hall. She opened the door. "Put one on and go. No one will even notice you're gone," she said, as she schemed with me, sharing a smile of encouragement.

I looked at her, still unsure.

"Go," she said. "You've lived with regret long enough. Don't regret this too."

* * *

Mr. Contelli was wearing his coat, a red scarf wrapped around his neck, and was ready to head over to my parents' house when he answered the door.

"Is Michael home?" I asked. I was flustered, but there was something in his eyes that told me he sympathized with me at that moment.

"Let me tell him you're here, Annabelle. I think he was just going into the shower," he said. He was doing his best to make me feel comfortable.

He disappeared upstairs to check and then came back down and escorted me into the library, a place I hadn't seen in a very long time. It looked the same, minus the couch under the window; the previously empty shelves were now fully stacked with hardback books and several knickknacks. I had always loved this place in the daytime; the way the light came streaming through the enormous picture windows that overlooked the Severn River added a sense of serenity to the place. The crystal chandelier centered over the desk added a touch of femininity to a mostly masculine room. It used to be Michael's favorite place in the house.

"He'll be down in a few minutes. He asked if you don't mind waiting," he said.

"Not at all."

"Okay," he said, as I attempted to search for any signs that he might still hold a grudge against me. "I'm going to head over now. I'll see you in a little while?"

"Yes, you will. Thank you very much."

The front door shut, and I heard his footsteps marching off across the path to the party.

I stood in the room near the desk and looked around. The Contellis' home was beautiful, I thought—much simpler than my parents' home, but with great detail. The fireplaces were etched, the walls showcased stunning crown molding, big and thick, and the floors were worn old pine, with dings and imperfections that gave them character. It was subtle but elegant. The middle drawer in the desk once housed our personal keepsakes—Michael's sketches, my poetry, our letters. I wondered if our items were still in there. It was always known as "Michael's drawer," and others were asked to "keep out." I fashioned myself in the seat of the desk, and slowly opened the drawer. Deep in the back of it, behind a small box of rubber bands, staples, and dried up Elmer's glue, was a shallow, old cigar box. I could still hear the murmur of shower water running, so I pulled it out.

It was just as I remembered it. The colors may have been a little faded, but it was still filled with some of our memorabilia. I felt like an intruder, but curiosity consumed me. There were charms and stickers, postcards and photographs. I noticed all the letters had been opened, and I started to peruse them. The first letter was from Michael to me when he had first been accepted at NYU. It read,

> Dear Annabelle,
> Can you believe it? I'm so excited. I've always wanted to live in New York. I can't wait for you to visit.
> —Love, Michael

The second one I examined was from me to him; my sophomoric poetry back then was something that belonged shoved in a box in the back of a desk. It pained me to read it.

And then I came across an unopened letter addressed to me from London. There was postage on it, but it had not been mailed.

I stared at it for seconds, minutes. My hands were shaking and I grabbed the letter opener. I knew it was wrong, but I gently opened it, trying to keep it as intact as possible, and unfolded the letter.

Dear Annabelle,

It's been nearly a year since you left me distraught at the airport and I'm still hoping you'll explain it to me. I'm in London now. I've been working at a newspaper in London; the position doesn't even have a formal title. My master's program is going well so far. I'm convinced this was a good decision. I muddle through without you, though it doesn't feel the same. I think it would have been great to experience all of this together.

I hope this letter reaches you at a time when you've been able to think clearly about what happened and can explain to me why you did what you did. It hurt, Annabelle; it still does. Any communication from you would be welcome. I really want to understand. I'm still so angry, I can't see straight, and some days I'm so mad I don't know what to do other than to throw myself into my work. But if I did this to you, if the shoe had been on the other foot, wouldn't you want to know why? Wouldn't you deserve and require an explanation?

I always assumed we meant more to each other than what has become of us.

Despite it all, I love you…always,

—Michael

I stared at it, the words beginning to blur as tears rolled down my face, ashamed, embarrassed, guilty and disgusted at the way I'd hurt him. I was crying because of the love I had let go of and never had the guts to attempt to rectify. Reading his words—his thoughts—was agonizing. A lump sat in my throat, and I stood as I heard his footsteps approaching from the hallway.

"Sorry to keep you waiting," he said cheerfully as he entered the room, rubbing his hands together, with a forced smile on his face. "I just needed to…"

He abruptly stopped speaking and looked at me quizzically when he saw me standing there crying, the letter in hand. I collapsed into the chair.

"I'm so sorry," I said, barely choking the words out through tears, unable to look him in the eyes. "I'm so sorry, Michael."

Michael

Annabelle was sobbing so violently, it was difficult to console her. She kept saying she was sorry, and I saw the letter in her hand. It was the one I had never mailed, the one I should have sent. I'd sealed it and never reopened it. The last time I was home visiting two years ago, I'd traveled with it in my briefcase and put it in my box in the desk. Call me sentimental—I couldn't throw it away, but I didn't want to open it and read it again either.

"Breathe," I told her, "it's okay." I was saying anything just to get her to calm down.

She swiveled the chair to look at me, and I knelt down before her, my hands on her lap, her hands on my forearms. She was looking down at me, and one of her tears landed on my sleeve, a remnant of mascara along with it gracing my blue shirt. We both noticed it.

"I'm sorry about that too," she said, staring at the watery, black drop.

She took deep, deep breaths at my urging, and grabbed another tissue off the desk to pat her eyes.

"I have so much to say to you, so much explaining to do, and so much forgiveness to ask you for, I don't even know where to begin," she said. I was looking at her. It felt like no time had passed; it felt like years had passed. She tugged at my soul without even trying.

"Then you're in luck," I said, "because I have all the time in the world to listen."

When I stood up after bending down in front of her, I got a little off balance and held onto the edge of the desk. "Fancy a drink?" I asked, trying to lighten the mood a bit as we headed for the family room.

I heard her heels on the hardwoods and knew she was right behind me. My mother had left the Christmas lights on in the house, and I noticed the dichotomy of the dimness and sparkle created an ambiance better suited for a night of romance rather than a more serious conversation that might take place between two old lovers.

I was trying to find the corkscrew to open a bottle of wine, searching among my mother's vast amount of drawers. Annabelle was still sniffling; I didn't want to look at her because I knew she was trying to get herself together. All this time, I'd been focused on what I deserved, on what I thought I was owed. Hearing the quiver in her voice and seeing the emotions she'd kept inside her gave me a pang of deep guilt, something I hadn't felt until now where our relationship was concerned. I finally found the corkscrew and opened the bottle. I pulled two wine glasses from the cabinet and poured some into each glass, but inadvertently knocked one of the wine glasses sideways and spilled it all over the counter. This got her attention. She grabbed a dishtowel and handed it to me. I made a second attempt to pour the wine again. I was successful.

I handed her a glass as she continued to try to maintain her composure. She took another deep breath and her eyes met mine. We walked over to the sofa where she placed her drink on the table, adjusted her dress, and began.

"I've sort of rehearsed this in my mind for years now. I've wanted to talk to you, see you, and now, here you are, and it almost hurts me to look at you, because I know how you must despise me—and my actions—and you have every right to. But I just wanted to say to you that I should never have done what I did, and I never, ever should have behaved in that manner. I got scared and

I panicked. I guess I thought you wouldn't understand, when in hindsight, you probably would have understood better than anyone. But leaving you at the airport with no way to contact me and no way of letting you know if I were alive or dead, that's unforgive-able, I know. However, what I'm most sorry for is that…"

She began to get weepy again and had to pause for a moment to collect herself.

"I'm most sorry that I hurt you. I realized it when I got home—I went to Vivi's, and she helped me sort it out. I had to muster up the courage to face you. I know I took too long. I drove back here to talk to you, but you'd left earlier in the day to go to London, and rightly so. I mean, why would you wait around for me? After I read the letter you left for me, I figured you would be better off without me. I'm sorry I didn't try to explain it then, and I'm also sorry that I've let ten years go by without an apology. Can you forgive me for what I did?"

I was having trouble looking at her eyes—they were full of pain and anguish. It made me wonder who suffered more as a result of it all.

"This is bringing up a lot of old feelings. I mean, who would have thought that we would be having this conversation all these years later?" I said.

She nodded, looking for forgiveness.

"I won't lie and say it didn't hurt. And I won't lie and say I un-derstood any of it. But I can tell you now that so much time's gone by and so much has changed me—and probably you too—that I forgive you. We don't always know why things happen the way they do or how it all becomes a bloody mess. But bloody messes do work out."

She stared at me as she continued to clutch the letter in her hand.

"Why didn't you send it?" she asked, pointing to it.

"Anger. Disbelief. I think those two feelings got in the way of me mailing it off to you."

"I wish you had."

She reached for her drink, her hand trembling as she lifted it to her lips. When she put it down, there were remnants of her lipstick on the rim. I wasn't sure what I should say or do next. I was in awe of this moment. Silence hung in the air. We were both still visibly emotional and felt awkward.

She put her wine glass on the table and stood, straightening her dress.

"So, thank you, then, for listening to me. I guess I'd better get back over before people start talking. Not that they won't talk when they see my puffy eyes," she said, pointing to them.

"I'd still like to come, if that's okay," I said.

She walked over to me and gently grabbed my forearm—and my sleeve—and brought it up to her eyes for examination.

"Of course," she said, "but you may want to change this lovely shirt I've destroyed with my blubbering."

* * *

When we came through the door, Annabelle snuck upstairs to fix her makeup and put Visine in her eyes to hide that she'd been weepy. I made my way to the great room in a new shirt, still a little stunned not just by what happened, but how I was feeling because of what happened. Everyone was mingling and laughing, sharing drinks and stories. I nonchalantly kept watch for her, though it seemed she was taking a long time to reappear. I was convinced that those who knew us well were watching us, trying to get a pulse on the situation. It was reminiscent of the old days when we felt like we were in a fish bowl.

Annabelle's father was at the bar making a batch of Mistletoe Martinis when Annabelle emerged from the hallway. We each took one from the bar and began moving about the room. In minutes I was on one side and she was on another. I was seeing people I hadn't seen in years, and was able to catch up on families and stories.

Vivi tapped me on my shoulder. "Well, look at you, all grown up and looking handsome," she said, and reached to give me a hug.

"And look at you!" I said, as I hugged her back. "You look exactly the same as when I left you."

"I knew there was a reason I always liked you, Michael," she said. "How've you been?"

"Not too bad, I have to say. I really loved it in London. Loved the people and loved living in the city. My job wasn't too shabby, either. It was a good experience for me. It's interesting to be home, though," I said.

"I'm sure it isn't easy to leave something you love behind," she said.

"It's never easy," I said.

I saw Annabelle make eye contact with Vivi, and they smiled at each other despite being at opposite ends of the large kitchen. Just then, I felt a hard smack on the back.

"Well, I've got to tell you, Mike, having you home makes this a very special Christmas," Annabelle's father said. Mr. Marco and I were always pretty tight, and he was unabashedly glad to see me.

"The tree turned out well, don't you think?" he said, turning to Vivi. "Michael helped me get it off the car and into the garage." Vivi nodded and gave Annabelle another look, like maybe she should come over and join the conversation.

"So, what are you going to do with yourself now that you're home?" he asked me.

"Actually, I'm moving to New York in a few weeks," I said. "I got a job working for a publisher."

"Wow! Big news! Your father didn't tell me that!" Gil said.

"Well, it was just confirmed, and he probably doesn't want to admit I'm leaving again," I said, "but my mother is chomping at the bit to see a show in the Theatre District."

"I'm sure she is," Gil said.

He turned to my mother who was standing a few feet away. "Carol. Carol! You didn't tell me Michael's moving to New York!" My mother joined the conversation, and I noticed Annabelle was also hearing this news for the first time. She disappeared into another conversation in the dining room. She was out of my line of sight.

"Yes, he is," my mother said, proud as a peacock. I'd forgotten how it felt to have your parents gloat over your successes, both the little and the big ones. It was somewhat embarrassing and uncomfortable; I wasn't used to that kind of attention. I never got it at work—I was always a behind-the-scenes kind of employee. Spotlight recognition never came my way, and I never minded that it didn't.

Vivi asked what part of the city I'd be working in, and I told her I'd be in Midtown, but that my apartment was most likely going to be in the West Village.

"Our group of seniors takes two trips a year up on the bus: one in the spring, and one in the fall. We spend the day in Midtown usually, seeing shows and shopping along 5th Avenue," she said.

In the midst of all this commotion, I scanned the room for

Annabelle. Although we were not patched up as neatly as she may have expected, and though I was still feeling unsettled over it, I wondered if she were okay. I excused myself, blaming it on needing another drink and tried to find her, but she was nowhere in sight. I scanned the entire downstairs and didn't see her anywhere.

"Do you need some food, Michael?" Mrs. Marco asked me.

"Oh, no thank you, Mrs. Marco." She stopped me and grabbed my arm. "Michael, I don't mind that you don't want any food, but I do mind that you're still calling me Mrs. Marco. At this point in our lives, I think it's safe to call me by my first name."

"Okay, Donna," I said.

"And please call Mr. Marco Gil. It's just silly now."

"Got it."

"Are you sure you don't want some eggplant parmesean?"

"Maybe in a little bit," I said.

"Where's Annabelle?" her mother asked.

"I'm not sure. I haven't seen her in a while," I said.

"Well, if you see her, tell her the eggplant I made for her in particular is ready to eat."

"Will do," I said. "By the way, Donna, I'm glad you're feeling better and sorry you had a tough go of it."

"Thank you, Michael. It's good to be alive," she said.

She continued mingling with her guests and playing hostess, which had always been her gift. It was difficult for me to imagine her sick with cancer, not knowing if she were going to live or die. I imagined it had been a horrible time for Annabelle, too, and that she was probably the glue that held the family together during it. I looked for her again, and then stepped outside wondering if she needed some fresh air.

I smelled cigarette smoke in the distance, so I walked out back and down by the path that led to the docks. It was freezing out, and the wind was beginning to whip.

"Annabelle?"

"Oh, I see you've caught me, I'm afraid," she said, as she stomped out her cigarette.

"What is this? Still a closet smoker?"

"Not as much as I use to be, but occasionally I like to light one up," she said. "It's not a habit, just an occasional stress reliever. We all have our vices, I suppose."

"That's true," I said, "some worse than others."

She pulled a mint out of her coat, unwrapped it, and plopped it in her mouth. Then she sprayed herself with the smallest bottle of perfume I'd ever seen, trying to camouflage her act.

"No need to invite suspicion," she said. "I don't need my mother harping on me. I'd offer you a mint, but it's my last."

"No problem. I'm about to sample your mother's eggplant. Why don't you join me? I'm hungry. Aren't you? She said she made it in your honor."

"Yes, she does make it especially for me," she said. "I'm not really hungry, but I could sit with you."

"Come on," I said, trying to leave the heaviness behind. It was Christmas Eve, after all. "If I'm not mistaken, I think we have about ten years of living to catch up on."

"Actually, that would be ten years and four months," she said, "but who's counting?"

Annabelle

Christmas Eve was not going to be remembered as the best or the worst, but rather as the one that allowed me to move forward, truly, for the first time since I had destroyed my relationship with Michael. Looking back, I can see how it hung over me—a cloud of melancholy that never exactly went away—lingering. There was always a sense of sadness lurking beneath the surface. I was confident Michael meant it when he said he could forgive me, and there was a lot of guilt I lived with, so I was trying to leave it behind. I didn't want to allow myself to become emotional again, and made a decided attempt to enjoy what was left of the evening.

I didn't mean to become bothered by what I'd overheard: that Michael had accepted a job in New York with a publisher and was going to move. I sat across from him at the dining room table as he savored every bite of my mother's eggplant. He and I both loved it; it had always been our favorite meal. He used to prefer dishes with meat. In fact, in the past he would have sold his soul for hot Italian sausage on a hard roll with peppers and onions. I wondered what his favorite food was now. Did he still drink five cups of coffee in the evenings when he needed to stay up late and get his work done? How many restaurant matchbooks numbered his collection? Would he still show his enthusiasm for boating as he rode the river in his dad's boat? Did he still espouse that Steinbeck ranked second only behind Dickens?

I was watching him eat as I continued sipping the potent martini my dad had concocted. It was starting to go to my head. I'd lost count as to how many I'd had, but I knew I needed to stop where I was. Just the slightest amount of alcohol could affect me. He saw me watching him eat and pointed to his dish.

"Are you sure you don't fancy any?" he asked me.

"Did you just say 'fancy'? We don't say that word here in America."

"You're making fun of me," he said, then cleared his throat. "Do you want some?" he said slowly, using a deliberate, low-pitched, mocking voice. I smiled.

"Some what?" I said, mimicking him. I was getting sloppy, and he chuckled at it.

"Eggplant?"

"No."

I got up, walked around the table, and handed him a napkin.

"You've got a little red sauce on your face," I said.

* * *

By the night's end, we were sitting near each other on the sofa listening to our families and friends as they sang Christmas carols. Vivi was playing the baby grand. They were all off key. No one but Carol could carry a tune, and we were trying to stifle our laughter. It was difficult to have a conversation among the hair-raising noise of the singers. I lured Michael away by tempting him with a cannoli.

"When I was in London, the only pasticceria worth a damn was in West London, and the cannolis didn't taste half as good as your mother's do," Michael said.

"That's too bad, though there aren't many around here either. I think my mom corners the market on Italian pastries."

He bit into a large, stuffed cannoli, its filling spilling over, the mini chocolate chips that were adhered to its brown shell breaking into pieces, making a mess all over his plate. Pieces fell out of his mouth, and the white ricotta cheese mixture decorated his upper lip and chin.

"Why can't she make these things easy to eat?" he asked.

For the first time that night, I laughed. I couldn't remember the last time I laughed that hard. It felt good.

Michael

It was Christmas morning and the house was quiet. The sun was tucked behind the heavy, fluffy winter clouds. The forecast called for snow flurries. Kids were probably excited by the thought. Being able to go out and play in the snow on Christmas was a big thrill for children. I remembered wishing for it as a kid myself. I hoped for their sakes a little snowfall would come their way.

We didn't leave the Marcos until one-thirty in the morning. Mr. Marco—Gil—had the booze flowing so freely that everyone loosened up and had a great time. The house was filled with noise, that's for sure. Christmas carols, gift exchanges, and games kept the evening light, fun, and engaging. It was nice to see everyone; it had been such a long time since I'd seen many of the people who'd attended. I'd come home for Christmas before. However, needless to say, I hadn't spent it with Annabelle's family and friends in years.

If I were to be perfectly honest, I wasn't sure what to make of the night with her. I tried not to drink too much because I didn't want anything to be distorted or misconstrued, so instead I gorged myself on Donna's tremendous spread of food. What started off as a touching apology ended up morphing into the two of us sitting side by side most of the night and talking, though I suspected she had one too many martinis and was definitely much more relaxed than she was at the beginning of the night.

At one point, when Annabelle had talked about her mother, and in particular, how stressful dealing with her mother's cancer had been for the family, she leaned over and put her hand on my thigh.

"I didn't have anyone to talk to," she told me, "so do you believe this? I started seeing a therapist. No one but my colleague Vicki—who sent me to her in the first place—knows I see one."

When the cannoli dropped onto my plate and the filling went all over my face, I couldn't help but laugh, but I was mostly laughing at the way she was laughing. It reminded me of what we had once.

I had no idea what the future would hold. I couldn't even predict the next week, the next month, or the next year. I didn't know what it all meant, but as a thirty-two-year-old man, I had learned something about myself over the course of those twenty-four hours: I had the ability not only to forgive, but also to recognize my own faults.

She ran away, but then again, so did I.

Annabelle

We were supposed to go to mass, but my head was throbbing.

"Mom—" I called, "—don't you have any Tylenol?"

My mother shuffled into the bathroom where I was scouring the cabinets for the drug. She looked a little rough, and her hair was sticking straight up, a direct result of bed head and too much fun. Ever since she'd been cancer-free, she'd been living each day as if it were her last. I couldn't say I blamed her for it. We looked at each other and start to giggle.

"That was some party," she said, looking at herself in the mirror and talking to her own reflection, aghast. "Look at me!"

I kissed her on the cheek and gave her a hug. "You threw a great party, Mom. Merry Christmas. It's going to be a nice one today."

"Yes," she told me, "but first we need to find the Tylenol and have some breakfast."

Vivi was already downstairs flipping pancakes, the coffee pot brewing. Knowing her, she'd probably been up since the crack of dawn and already had most of the mess downstairs cleaned up. She was listening to Dean Martin's Christmas album in the CD player, so she was happy. All that was left to put away were some of the chaffing dishes and the wine glasses that she had hand-washed and set upside down on a towel to dry next to the sink.

"Well, well," she said, inspecting my mother and me, "look what the cat dragged in." She was wearing my mother's Christmas apron, lifting pancakes onto plates for us. "You two need to get a little food in your system."

We sat down at the table and my father emerged, already

shaved, showered, and ready to go.

"Who's hungry?" he asked, and then kissed my mother, Vivi, and me and wished us a Merry Christmas. He sat down at the table, and Vivi offered him a plate.

They were all looking at me, as if they were waiting for the story from last night.

"What?" I said.

"Well, what happened with Michael?" my mother asked. "Come on! You've got to tell us something!"

Vivi raised her eyebrows from the stove and gave a cautionary look. Perhaps it was a warning to heed.

"Not this time, you all," I said, shaking my head and smirking. "Not this time."

We attended mass as a family, something that was rare for us. While I certainly had my beliefs, I didn't go as regularly as I should, and neither did my parents until my mother was ill. When my mother became well, she vowed to go more regularly, and that she has done. We headed over to their parish, St. Mary's, for Christmas mass. I scanned the congregation for Michael and his parents, but I didn't see them.

My stomach was in knots. I did "make merry," but it was more so because I had butterflies, a sensation I hadn't experienced for quite some time. I had taken two bites of my pancakes earlier, and I had no desire to eat at all. My emotions were jumbled, intermixed with happiness, some sentimentality, and anxiety over what might unfold, though I had absolutely no right to hold any hopeful expectations of my relationship with Michael. He was moving to New York, and I knew that wasn't conducive to rebuilding any sort of friendship or relationship.

As the homily winded down, I remembered the last Christmas

we had spent together. We had been dreaming of taking a vacation to Italy—Rome, Florence, Venice, Siena—and had been looking at books, reading up on the trip, when he surprised me with a little package under the tree.

"I got something for you," he said, handing me the beautifully wrapped gift.

"What is this?" I asked.

"Something for you to have for all of our trips."

I opened the Tiffany-blue wrapping to find a sterling charm bracelet with a single charm on it. It was a Roman coin and on the back it read, in very small, engraved letters: *Our journey. XO.*

"So, does this mean we're going to go?" I asked.

"That's what I'm hoping," he said. "Sometime next year—maybe next Christmas. And then with every trip we'll take together, we'll add a charm onto it. Do you like it?" he asked, somewhat pleased with himself that he'd given me such a thoughtful gift.

I'd kissed him then, wrapping my arms around him like I'd never let him go.

The unfortunate thing was that bracelet remained tucked away in my jewelry box, still adorned with only a single charm, and no trip to attach to its memory.

* * *

Christmas dinner consisted of ham and lasagna, a tradition in our family, and Vivi's mouth-watering bean dish with almonds. Afterwards, we exchanged a few gifts, brewed a pot of tea, set the Christmas cookies on the coffee table, and the four of us played Scattergories.

I decided to sleep over for a second night. At nine we popped in our VHS copy of "It's A Wonderful Life," and I thought to myself that mine really wasn't so bad.

* * *

In the morning, I collected my belongings, kissed Vivi goodbye, thanked my parents for a wonderful Christmas, and headed back to my condo. It was a Sunday, and the city was sleepy the day after the holiday. I was so tired that I thought I might actually be able to sleep. I hadn't taken a nap in so long, I wasn't sure I'd even know how to do it.

I parked in the parking lot and opened my trunk to gather my small overnight bag and the bag of presents I received. I shut the trunk and walked up the flight of stairs to my second-floor condo, and I saw him there, scribbling some kind of note and trying to attach it to my door.

"Cole?"

He was startled. "Annabelle," he said, taking the note off the door and shoving it into his pocket. "I was just leaving you a note."

"What are you doing here?" I asked.

"I was hoping we could talk for a minute?"

I wasn't sure I wanted to let him in, but it was freezing, the temperature hovering somewhere around twenty degrees. I put my luggage and bag down and wrestled with my keys as I tried to dig them out of my coat pocket.

"Sure," I said. He looked different, and I wasn't sure why. The knit cap he was wearing was almost covering his eyes.

"Come on in," I said, as I unlocked the door with my key. He walked in leaving my things behind and started to take off his coat and hat. I grabbed my bags and brought them in myself, setting them next to the door. Typical.

"Nice place," he said, looking around, sizing it up. "Better than our place in Baltimore."

I took off my coat and turned up the heat on the thermostat. It was cold inside because I'd lowered the temperature before I left. "Do you want something warm to drink? Hot chocolate, coffee, tea?"

"Whatever you're making is fine with me," he said.

He was unusually amenable, yet seemed jittery. I kept my eyes on him because I was sensing something was not right. I put the kettle on the stove and returned to the living room. Then I sat and asked him to do the same.

"So, what's going on?" I asked.

"My life's a mess," he said. "I think I might lose my job and I'm having a hard time being happy since you left. I don't even know if I can pay my rent." How had I not seen it before? Always a mess. Always requiring attention. I found it so unattractive.

Oh, God, I thought. He was going to do this to me again. He needed something. I was determined not to allow him to make me feel guilty about his stupidity, his juvenile behavior. Somewhere in there might have been a nice guy, but it would take quite a reformation. Unfortunately, his selfishness was unparalleled. I pitied the woman who got him next.

I made no response, but instead got up when the teakettle whistled. I made us each hot chocolate—I was in the mood for it, though I was sure he preferred some Baileys or Schnapps added into it. I brought the mugs over and placed them on my New York coasters I had bought in the Village with Michael many moons ago.

"So, what does this mean, all these dilemmas?" I asked. I heard myself say it, and I sounded like Delia.

"I don't know," he said. "I don't know how to make it better."
It was always about him.

"Well, I do. I know. You just won't want to hear what I have to say. We've been over it a thousand times."

He ran his fingers through his blonde, straight hair, his hairline more receded than it had been before, and it became messy. He was an attractive guy—empirically there was no doubt about it. He got plenty of female attention. The problem was, once you got to know him and all his baggage, he became less and less attractive. I questioned my own judgment. How had I allowed myself to be intimate with him? The thought eluded me now.

"Go ahead," he said.

"You're in a repetitive cycle and only one person can fix it, Cole, and that's you. You drink too much and you can't commit to anything, let alone a job. You bounce from one thing to another, never satisfied. You're uncaring—I mean, look what you did when my mother was sick. How you treated me. How you cheated on me during it. I don't trust a word you say to me, and unfortunately, I never will again, because you repeatedly do things to please your-self, never considering the feelings of others. We should never have lived together. When I look back now, I realize that I was never happy. You didn't make me happy. And you know why? Because you think of no one but yourself."

He sat there blankly staring ahead.

"I messed up with you, Annabelle. You're the best thing that ever happened to me. I just couldn't see it." There he goes again, I thought. I'd heard it all before. It was almost masterful the way he could pile it on.

I corrected him. "I'm going to say something that could be very hurtful, Cole, and for that, I'm sorry. You may believe that I was the best thing for you, but I'm certain that you were not the best thing for me. You hurt me too many times; there were too many lies time and time again. I forgave you twice, but I'm not the one for you, Cole, and quite frankly, until you get yourself straightened out, you're going to have a hard time finding someone who is."

I had hit a nerve.

"That's some rotten shit you're saying to me," he said, standing up, snatching his coat off the arm of the chair, almost knocking it over. "I don't know why I came here."

He headed for the door and reached for the door handle. I hoped he'd opened it to leave, but he didn't. He turned back around and charged at me like a bull, his face red with anger.

"You know what, Annabelle, you can sit on your little pedestal and criticize everyone else, but you're not perfect. You've made mistakes in the past. I know. I read your little journal that day about you and Michael and all that crap that went on between you. I'm not perfect, but neither are you—" He was pointing his finger in my face.

"How dare you? How dare you come here asking me for my help? Where the hell were you when I needed you? Where were you when my mother was sick? We both know where you were, and it wasn't with me. We have nothing—nothing—Cole!" I swallowed hard and opened the door.

"Get out!" I had no need of him anymore.

He looked at me, and started to raise his arm; for a moment I feared he might hit me, but he didn't. Instead, he mumbled "righteous bitch" and slammed the door behind him. I heard his heavy footsteps plod down the steps. When the engine of his car started, I listened for him to pull away, and it went quiet.

My neighbor next door had been in the hallway and heard the

commotion. He peeked his head around the door to see if everything was okay and asked if I wanted to call the police.

"Not yet," I told Jonathan. "But if he ever comes back again, I will. An ex," I said, still rattled. "Some people never seem to go away."

Jonathan told me he had an extra dead bolt in his toolbox, that I was welcome to it, and that he'd be happy to install it for me. I took him up on his offer, and within minutes, he had it in working order. There was only one outside entrance into my place, minus the second floor balcony, and it was the door, so I was thankful. Jonathan was a retired military officer, and it was comforting to have him as my neighbor. His wife was a former teacher and worked at the library.

"We've been meaning to invite you over for dinner," Jonathan said. "Maybe next year," he joked.

"That would be nice," I said, as we parted ways at the door. I wanted nothing more than to lock myself inside my condo, but had an unusual sense of discomfort about being alone. I thanked him again, disappeared inside, locked the bolt tightly, and unpacked my things.

Cole had always been threatened by Michael; or better yet, he was threatened by the thought of Michael. They'd never met, but through my friends, Cole knew of our relationship and understood the seriousness of it. When he said that he'd actually read the words I'd written about my life with Michael in my journal, I felt violated. Those were my thoughts, and my sentiments about my heartbreak over Michael. I guarded that journal so well, and kept it beside my bed in an old trunk with a key. I never knew he had read it.

Admittedly, I never stopped writing in that journal, and, therefore, I had a confession to make. I started writing in it when I was seventeen and continued to do so. Until I started to see Delia, it was the only place where I could make sense of and rationalize what I did to Michael. Writing my thoughts and emotions down was how I communicated and confessed my often-debilitating regret. If Cole had indeed read it, he would have read things that would have made him feel insecure. He would have understood that I never quite recovered. That much was clearly scribed.

The grandfather clock was ticking almost as loudly as my heart was pounding. A revelation occurred to me: Could Cole have distanced himself from me little by little because he was never sure if I loved him? His patterns of behavior were clear: he pulled away, drank, and then, was unfaithful. It wasn't always awful. We had a few good months together in the beginning.

I was left with the understanding that only two people in the world had read my journal. I was one; the other was Cole. He would not have been my second choice.

Nevertheless, I refused to take on the role of the martyr where he was concerned. Generally speaking, he wasn't the nicest person. His self-absorption was remarkable at times, and his actions were hardly justifiable. But when I could see the bigger picture, I was left with a disturbing realization, and one that I hadn't contemplated before.

Cole had a temper, as was evidenced by the surprise visit. I settled in on the sofa and tried to distract myself with a book I was reading. It had been hours since he'd left, but I was still rattled by it.

I fell asleep on the couch, and when I awoke, made my way to the shower. I was blow-drying my hair when the telephone rang. It was Will.

"So, did you get engaged?" I asked him.

"What do you think?" he asked.

"I'm guessing that's a no."

"Bingo," he said. "How was your Christmas?"

"Very nice until this morning when Cole showed up at my door." I told him what transpired, and he was genuinely worried about me.

"I think you should call the police." He started to make me nervous about the situation.

"And say what? That he wanted to talk to me?"

"I guess you have a point. He didn't really do anything but get mad."

"That's right," I said, as I tried to convince myself to believe the same.

"Do you want to meet for dinner or something?" he said. "Or I could come hang out, bring my baseball bat."

"I don't know. I'll call you in a little bit. You'll be home?"

"Yes," he said, "waiting breathlessly for your call."

Michael

It was Sunday night, and I felt like I needed to get out of the house. I called Andrew and asked him if he wanted to meet somewhere for a beer. He told me Sarah and he were attending a concert in D.C., so I decided to venture out alone. There was a basketball game on, so I figured I'd sit at the bar at Riordan's and get a burger and a beer. It was a good Irish place with exposed brick and lots of personality.

There was an open seat at the bar, so I grabbed it. The redheaded bartender looked like she might speak with an Irish brogue, but instead sported a thick Brooklyn accent; she convinced me to order the corned beef sandwich instead of a burger.

The guy next to me leaned over and said, "She actually knows what she's talking about. The corned beef is really fantastic here."

"Thanks," I said, noticing he was watching the game. He was wearing a flannel shirt and jeans, and his dark-rimmed glasses seemed a little too big for his face. "Who are you pulling for?"

"Wizards," he said. "You?"

"Same."

The bartender brought me a beer and I took a swig. I was glad for the change of scenery. I needed to feel the pub atmosphere. Reminded me of London.

"I don't know," the guy said, "I don't think this team's going anywhere for a while. I'm convinced they're cursed. Every move they make goes badly."

"They haven't been good for years," I said, happy to make conversation.

There were quite a few people in the place. It was crowded, and despite the fact that the bar area was hopping, the service was top notch. After a few minutes passed, the bartender brought out two corned beef sandwiches and gave one to each of us.

"I see you ordered the same."

"Exactly the same," he said. "Outstanding."

He seemed like a decent guy, so we conversed throughout our dinner, as we remarked on the ineptitude of the team and its inability to make any three-pointers.

"This is why I can't write about sports," he said. "I'd get too emotional about it and write something damning."

"You're a writer?" I asked.

"Yeah. I write for the local newspaper and I'm a freelancer for some other national publications. I mostly write features. You?"

"I used to be a writer, but then became an assistant editor of a paper. I'm off to New York next week to start working for a nonfiction publishing house."

"Cool—I mean that," he said, nodding, smiling, and chewing his food simultaneously.

"Thanks."

The game was going worse for the Wizards than we could both stand, so we switched topics. He mentioned that he lived in a house in the city.

"Where is it?" I asked.

"About seven blocks from here. I love it. I can walk pretty much everywhere—including to the paper."

"That's a plus," I said. "It's a selling point to living in a city. Proximity to everything and two legs that work." He laughed.

The bartender gave us another round and the air in the bar filled with smoke. It reminded me of the pubs in London.

"Jesus!" he said. "Can anyone handle the ball on this team?"

We chatted on about writing and he told me about his girlfriend and how she wasn't always understanding of his journalistic career. "Sometimes I have to travel for work and she hates that," he said. "It's been a bit of a sticking point in our relationship."

"Well," I said, "all relationships have sticking points, don't they? You just have to get past them."

"I guess," he said, and took a monstrous bite out of his corned beef.

"You know," he continued with his mouth full, "it's true. All relationships do have sticking points, it's just some are bigger than others. I guess mine's not insurmountable."

"I'd say not," I said.

"In fact, one of my friends—who I tried to convince to come out with me tonight for dinner and the reason why I'm alone—is having a tough time. Her old boyfriend showed up on her doorstep today trying to harass her, practically threatening her with vio- lence. Plus, her former fiancé is back in town, and she's living with guilt over something that happened ten years ago. I'm one of her best friends, and she never told me the full story about her for- mer fiancé until recently. Kept it all inside. She can't get a break, I swear. I should be thankful I only have Linda's petty complaint about my travel to moan about."

The coincidence was too strong, so I prodded him. I stopped eating.

"What's your friend's guilt?"

"She left the guy at the airport on the day they were supposed to run off and get married. She's never forgiven herself, poor thing. I'm not much of a psychologist, but I think it's why she hasn't really moved on. If you ask me, she was probably only with her former boyfriend to punish herself. There was never anything good there. He was always a selfish ass. No one liked him."

I stared at this man, and made a deduction. He was obviously an intimate friend, and because he appeared to be incredibly genuine and honest, it would have been dishonest of me to keep it from him. It didn't seem right.

"What's your name?" I asked, as I stuck my hand out for a proper shake.

"Will Gregory," he said.

"Hey, Will. I'm Michael Contelli."

He stared at me, and then made the connection.

"Get the hell out of here," he said.

* * *

Will was a good bloke. We left the bar, and I shoved the napkin with the address he had scrawled on it into my pocket. I wasn't entirely convinced what I was about to do was appropriate, but there was something bothering me about the situation Will had disclosed. Plus, Will had encouraged me to go and even offered to come along.

I was driving to a section of Annapolis where I'd never been—it was a newer development. I was also adjusting to driving the opposite way on American soil. I was a wee bit rusty. I wasn't exactly sure where I was going, but when I thought I had it right, I pulled into the parking lot and searched for number 207. It must have been located on the second floor. I didn't want to scare her. If she had a peephole, and if she were brave enough to use it, she'd see it was me.

I rang the doorbell and heard her scurrying around. I was hoping she was alone. When I heard the pitter-patter of her feet, I wasn't shy.

"Annabelle, it's Michael," I said somewhat loudly through the door.

I heard her unlock the chain; then I heard the slide of a lock. She opened the door.

"Hello," she said. She was wearing flannel pants and a t-shirt, her hair appeared to be a little damp, and her cheeks were rosy. She had a small blanket wrapped around her shoulders.

"Hi," I said. What was I thinking? It was a little uncomfortable.

"I'm in my pajamas," she said. "Hope you don't mind."

"Not at all."

The neighbor's door opened, and an older man stepped outside. "You okay, Annabelle?" he asked.

"Yes," she said. "Jonathan, this is an old friend of mine, Michael. All is well here," she said.

Jonathan and I exchanged a wave, and he nodded. "Just checking," he said.

"Thank you," she replied, and Jonathan disappeared and closed his door.

"Come on in," she said, and I stepped inside and looked around.

I heard her fuss with the deadbolt after she locked the door tightly behind her. The condo was warm, as the aroma of a cinnamon candle filled the air. The main area was pale yellow. She had good taste in decorating; it was very comfortable and cozy with tasteful French-inspired furniture. She always liked that. A movie had been paused on her television. There was a cup of something hot on her coffee table, a half-eaten bowl of popcorn on her *Vogue* magazine, and coasters were strewn across the table. They looked vaguely familiar.

"To what do I owe this surprise?"

"Honestly?"

"Of course. Why? Were you planning on deceiving me?" She smiled.

"Would you believe it if I said I was worried about you? And apparently your neighbor is, as well."

"How so?"

"I had the distinct pleasure of enjoying a very tasty corned beef sandwich with your mate Will tonight. The two of us noshed on some greasy food and ended up watching the Wizards game at Riordan's."

"Is that so?" She raised her eyebrows and digested this information. "Small world, huh?"

"Smaller than we can even imagine," I said. "He's a heck of a talker."

She crossed her arms, intrigued by the mystery that was this story as it unfolded before her very eyes.

"He told me your skint boyfriend showed up today and seemed a bit dodgy. We were both worried." She looked at me cockeyed.

"You're using those British words again, aren't you?"

"Ah. Quite right. Let me speak your language. Unstable, then. Your broke and somewhat unstable boyfriend's presence here today made us both uncomfortable."

"Ex-boyfriend," she clarified.

"Did you tell your folks about it?"

"No," she said. "I didn't want to worry them."

I didn't say anything, but I thought it was a bad idea to keep it from them; what if something had happened to her? The guy sounded like he had issues and was in a bad spot—especially if he was in need, as Will mentioned—and one never knew how a desperate person would react. But what the hell did I know.

"So your door's been bolted for safety?" I asked her.

She nodded. I wasn't sure how to broach the next question, so I decided to just be direct. "Are you expecting any company?"

"Who would be coming over at nine-thirty on a Sunday night?" she asked.

"I don't know. Just asking."

She shook her head. "Nope. No plans for any company until you showed up."

She smiled that crazy smile I had once loved, the one that used to mean she was up to something, the one that beamed when she was playful and flirtatious.

She ushered me inside, and I began to take off my coat.

"Let me get this straight," she said, as she sat down on the couch, lifted her knees up to her chin, and wrapped her arms around them. "You're planning on being my protector without asking first if it's okay with me?"

I thought for a second, and then I said, "Is it okay with you?"

She looked at me and grabbed the remote. "Does this mean I have to rewind back to the beginning of the movie and offer you some popcorn?"

"More than likely," I said.

* * *

I offered to help in the kitchen, but she declined the gesture and told me to make myself comfortable, so I did as she said. I supposed we had every intention of watching a movie, but then she appeared with a tray of wine and cheese. She had a small fire going in her fireplace and it was crackling while we talked.

I asked her about her job, something we hadn't discussed on Christmas Eve. She told me about the college, about the courses she taught and the students. We talked about Will and their friendship and how much the students loved when he visited. She told me how long it took her to get the Ph.D. and that she didn't regret a day of it.

Then she started to tease me, remembering my disdain for the Beat Generation and Jack Kerouac and how she considered him to be one of the most formidable writers of our time, which always ruffled my feathers. We had a cheeky debate, and I launched into the brilliance of Dickens and told her about his museum in London and how it had served as a source of inspiration for me when I first arrived. We talked about *The Times* and Albert and Janie and Billy.

"Do you still write?" she asked.

"You mean not for the paper? You mean my own stuff?"

"Yes," she said.

"A little. You?"

"A few bad pieces of poetry now and then. A couple of them made their way into an anthology."

"That's great," I said. "You'll have to show them to me."

"Maybe," she said. "It's not always easy sharing one's work."

"You're right about that. I've been working on some fiction. Sometimes I think it's dead and other times, I think it has potential."

"More wine?" she asked.

She poured a little more into my glass then tossed another log on the fire. It was snapping like crazy, and the wind howled outside rattling her sliding glass door.

"I saw Andie that night at the bar. Are you two still friends?" I asked in the midst of all this catching up.

"Yes," she said. "She just became engaged to Charlie—he owns one of the bars in Annapolis."

"Oh, he's Charlie! I didn't put 'Charlie's' and Charlie together," I said.

"Yes. That's Andie's Charlie. I should have talked to you that night. It just was so…"

"Awkward?" I said.

"Yes. Awkward," she said.

"It's not awkward now, right?"

"I don't feel it," she said, and I believed she meant it.

She played with her cracker and sipped her wine. She had no makeup on. Her hair was long—way past her shoulders. I'd always found Annabelle to be naturally beautiful. She may have been even more beautiful than I had remembered. Since we had cleared the air, she seemed more comfortable, and I knew I was, as well.

"So, tell me about this New York job," she said. I told her about the position, Dot Cranston, the office, and the flat—apartment—I'd just agreed to lease. She was somewhat impressed that I'd be editing nonfiction books.

"It sounds perfect for you," she said.

"We loved New York, right?"

"YOU loved it," she said, "and then I grew to love it."

"Some things take time," I said. There was a brief moment of silence, then I spoke. "May I use your loo?"

"There you go again. I need to purchase a British slang dictionary to keep up with these conversations."

She was still sitting in exactly the same position when I returned and was staring at the fire, the glow of it shining in her eyes, illuminating her olive skin.

"When's the last time you were in New York?" I asked.

She contemplated the question for a second, and then I knew. "Don't say ten years and four months."

She nodded and shrugged her shoulders. That one response ate at me, left me sad, hollow.

Annabelle

When I heard the knock last night, I panicked. Admittedly, I was worried. I made my way toward the door, with the phone in hand in case I needed to call Jonathan or the police. When I looked through the peephole, I saw Michael. Then I heard him call my name. I had barricaded myself in my condo concerned that Cole would return. I probably should have accepted Will's invitation to go out, but I was too afraid of what I might have found when I returned home. I realized that was paranoid thinking, though I may have been justified to be wary of him.

The clock read six-fifty in the morning. I tiptoed out of my bed and peeked out of the bedroom doorway to get a glimpse of the living room couch where I set Michael up with sheets, blankets, and a pillow. I saw his jeans, shirt, and socks draped over my velvet chaise and assumed he was sleeping in his "pants," as he called them. The covers were up around his neck, his head turned sideways on the pillow, and only his bare right foot was dangling out of the covers. I stood there and watched him sleep.

So much had happened that it was almost hard to believe he was here. I was grateful to him for coming by last night and was also hopeful that the gesture meant that I'd been forgiven and could finally put that part of my therapy behind me.

When Michael started to stir and he opened his eyes, I came out of my room as if I had just awakened, too, though I'd been sitting in the doorway watching him sleep for over an hour.

"Hi, sleepy," I said.

"Hey."

"How are you?"

"Good," he said. "I think my mere presence kept the bad guy away."

"Want some coffee? Breakfast?"

"Maybe in a little bit. This couch wasn't so bad," he said, sitting up and patting the cushions with his hand as he readjusted the pillows, his hair messy, his five o'clock shadow more visible than it had been as we sat in the dim light last night.

"What's your game plan today?" I asked. I was on my semester break, and he wasn't due to move just yet.

"I've got to head home. I have some calls to make and packing to organize," he said.

"You know what they say, though, right?" I said. He looked puzzled. "You can't do anything unless your body's been properly fueled for the day. Let's have breakfast."

"Ah, but how does your cooking compare to your mother's? Her eggplant was outstanding. Can your breakfasts measure up? I don't even know if I can trust you to cook or bake."

I stomped my foot and had to refrain from laughing. "What? Are you kidding me? How dare you question my culinary skills! Did I not put cheese and crackers on a plate and pour you some wine last night?"

"You did," he said. "It was amazing."

"I sense a tiny bit of sarcasm there. Nevertheless, you're in luck, because I'm not the best cook. Let's go to brunch at The Maryland Inn for old time's sake."

He grinned. "You got it. For old time's sake."

Michael

I had to wear my clothes from the night before. I wet my hair
in the bathroom to try to get it to stay down, and Annabelle dressed
in jeans, a sweater, and her boots. We bundled up and took the
walk together in the cold morning air. As we walked, sometimes
there was silence, and all I could hear were her heels clicking on
the pavement. I loved that sound.

The Maryland Inn wasn't too crowded; the churchgoers hadn't
bombarded the place yet. We were seated at a small table for two
in front of the brick fireplace while the quiet jazz band played in
the other room. The subtlety of the music added ambiance to the
already charming, historic space.

We helped ourselves to the filling buffet replete with eggs,
bacon, waffles, French toast, fresh fruit, crab cakes, salads, and
breads, pastries, and muffins of every kind.

"These pastries are good," I said, "but they don't hold a candle
to your mother's."

"Right," she said, "and don't tell her we came here."

I called my dad last night in the midst of the "protect Annabelle" operation just to be considerate and let him know I wouldn't
be home, that I was staying the night at Annabelle's. I didn't allow
him to ask anything, and he got it. But I knew I'd be bombarded by
questions later, one after another, when the home front firing squad
got a hold of me.

"So, are you worried that your ex will try to see you again?" I
asked.

"Yes," she said, "and no. I'm not sure what he will do. But
enough about him. Honestly. I'm through discussing him. It's one

of those relationships where you actually scratch your head and wonder what you were thinking."

She took a bite of her eggs and gently patted her lips with the napkin. "What happened with you and your ex-wife?" she asked. This was the first time she'd addressed it.

I thought it would be uncomfortable to discuss it with Annabelle, but her candor with regard to Cole made it easy.

"I can relate to what you just said about your ex. I didn't love her," I said plainly. It came out cold, unfeeling. I had to try to soften it. "We weren't right for each other from the start, and I should never have married her. There really is no more to the story," I said. "It was a mistake. It didn't last long, and the nature of it—or lack of it—really isn't worth mentioning."

She was looking into my eyes, a piercing concern emanating from her face. She put the fork on her plate and wiped her hands with the napkin. She reached for my hand and placed hers on top of it, letting it linger. For the first time in ten years, I felt her skin on mine.

"I'm sorry you had to go through that," she said. "I'm really sorry."

* * *

"So, it's off to New York then," she said as more of a question rather than a statement.

"Yes. It appears that is where I'm headed."

We were walking past the harbor and were headed toward the Eastport Bridge.

"How does Annapolis look to you?" she asked. "The same or different?"

We stopped at the top of the bridge, and I inspected the land-scape, taking it all in. The vantage point offered a clear view of the city.

"Yacht Club looks the same," I said. "This area on the Eastport side of the bridge looks a little different to me. And where you live, I've never been before."

"But overall, not much is different, right?"

"I would say you are correct in that assessment."

"I know," she said. "I do love it here. I put my name on the waiting list for a boat slip. We have a very small marina and a lim-ited number of slips. But I'd like to own a small one."

"You're kidding?" I said.

"Does that surprise you?" she asked, batting her eyes, clearly flirting with me.

"Actually, not at all," I said. "A powerboat, I presume."

"Is there any other kind of boat?" she teased.

We continued our walk back to her condominium. When we ar-rived, we stood near my car for a moment. It was difficult to know what to say.

"I hope I'll see you again soon, Michael," she said.

"Let's plan on it. I'll let you know when I'm settled."

She nodded and smiled. "That would be nice."

I reached over and gave her a hug. She squeezed me back. "I'll see you soon, then," I said. I put my keys in the door, and she stepped away as I got into the car. She stood there and waved to me as I pulled away, and I could still see her standing there in the rearview mirror as I exited her complex.

* * *

On my ride home, I couldn't help but recount what had just transpired. It would have been easy to fall back into step with Annabelle, but I knew that would require an inordinate amount of trust and understanding. I'd always have my guard up, and that wasn't exactly a healthy stance in any relationship. Quite frankly, if either of us thought it would be a rational notion to try it again, I don't know if I could. The idea of going through another disappointment and having it fail again was reason enough for both of us to stay far, far away from it. I convinced myself to be satisfied that the past was over, settled, and that it was time to move on. In what direction, I had absolutely no bloody idea.

She seemed vulnerable to me. She was more fragile than I remembered. It was probably the result of what she's had to deal with over the last few years. The stress of her mother's illness, in addition to the guy she'd saddled herself with, had changed her. I could tell there was a hole somewhere, and that part of her may be unreachable. Maybe I was overanalyzing it. Some of this was expected—we all change and have more responsibilities as we truly become adults—but her hole seemed a little deeper and wider than most. We shared some laughs last night, and her quick wit never ceased to amaze me, but I saw what Will had mentioned to me at the bar. She had a lot of distractions and disappointments to deal with, and not all of them had to do with me.

The reconnecting was good, even under the somewhat tenuous situation with her ex-boyfriend. I didn't want to harp on it, and I'd be lying if I said the idea of him in general didn't bother me. Talking like we did over wine brought back emotions that I thought—and for years had hoped—might be gone forever. And though we did share a few personal stories, what we mostly did was just reconnect. No lines were crossed, that's for sure.

The Annabelle I knew was still there somewhere, as I caught glimpses of it at times. Her sharp, punchy sense of humor always kept me on my toes. However, our interaction was much different from what I remembered it being in our younger days. What all this means, I don't know. There were things we knew for certain, and there were those things we couldn't even begin to know. I knew I was moving to New York and would take a new job. I didn't divulge too many details of my plans to her simply because I didn't entirely know what they were myself.

Could I deny that I still felt something for her? That I hadn't ever been able to put Annabelle completely out of my mind? I watched her talking, watched her hands, her eyes, her expressions, her mouth. She got to me. It was difficult to explain how or why. The pain I saw in her eyes on Christmas Eve left me no other path but to forgive her. It was much easier to do than I imagined.

And even though I told her I'd forgiven her, there was a part of me that wondered—really wondered—if that was all there was to it. Did it really come that easily? After I mulled it over on her couch at four in the morning, trying to get myself to sleep and relax, I wondered if I hadn't been kidding myself all these years. I'd blamed her for everything. I'd let the whole of the relationship and its failure rest on her shoulders. And yet, I did nothing—absolutely nothing—to remedy the situation. It was so much easier to be angry and blame her for it all. It was just that much easier.

* * *

When I walked through the door, my dad was sitting at the kitchen table getting ready to work a half-day. He was dressed casually, something I wasn't used to seeing when he headed for the office.

"What was going on last night with Annabelle?"

My mother magically entered the room, her ears alerted to the discussion. "Her old boyfriend showed up at her door yesterday dumping his misery on her, and I just went there in case…"

"To protect her?" my mother interrupted.

"What are you on about, Mom? I didn't have a shield or a gun. I just thought she might be scared."

"How did you know about it?"

"I met her friend Will, one of her best mates, when I was watching the game at the bar. He knew the story and told me."

My parents exchanged knowing glances and shared in the wonderment. I wouldn't permit them to play their games. I wasn't in the mood for it.

"You two know I'm moving to New York, right? This is total crap. We put an ugly past behind us and that's it. I won't say another word to you two about it. I'm going to take a shower," I said, frustrated, and left them and their gaping mouths to each other.

* * *

The next morning, my real estate agent needed me to sign some paperwork, so I boarded Amtrak again, bound for New York. I needed to finalize the details of the apartment and get my plans in order before I assumed a new job and responsibilities. I'd booked a hotel room for the next several days because I had to shop for some necessities. I had to arrange for the furniture I had in storage in Annapolis to be shipped to the city. As the train departed from Baltimore, I got a knot in my stomach. I hoped I was doing the right thing. All the way around.

Annabelle

I was enjoying time off from work, and was only slightly uncomfortable when I thought about the incident with Cole. Michael's presence in my home had relaxed me, because I was extremely anxious prior to his arrival at my door. I'd put the movie on to take my mind off things, though I'd probably seen it about twelve times. However, Michael's appearance provided the best therapy. Delia would have been pleased.

I owed Andie a call. I planned on taking her up on her idea of shopping together, and she knew nothing of my reconciliation with Michael. This made me feel like I'd been keeping it from her, which I wasn't. Plus, I was supposed to be attending an invitation-only party on New Year's Eve at Charlie's. I was permitted a guest, and I contemplated asking Michael to go, but I'd held off on that.

When I'd tidied up my apartment yesterday after Michael left, cleaning up dishes and putting presents away, I put everything back in its place minus the blanket on the couch, the one Michael slept underneath. I liked seeing it there, just the way he left it.

After I showered, I dialed Will at work. He picked up the phone after the first ring. "Will Gregory," he said.

"So, how'd you like Michael?"

"Yeah, that's one for the record books. I'm talking to him about you, and I don't know who the hell he is. I felt like an ass!"

"Why were you talking about me?"

"Oh, long story. That one has to be saved for one of our nights out. He seems pretty cool, though, Annabelle. I'm not sure I understand why you dumped him those many years ago."

"When you say 'dumped' like that, I sound like a bitch."

"Well…"

"That's enough of you," I said. "Michael is a great guy. The best one I know."

"Besides me, of course."

"Of course, that's a given," I said, and then I told him my version of what happened between us, leaving no detail out, laying it all out on the table and explaining to him why, standing on my balcony, a cup of coffee in my hand looking at the scenery that surrounds me, I felt differently today. I saw the world in its glorious hues of greens and blues, reds, browns, yellows, and whites, its sparkling lights and its crystal waters dancing beneath the sky. The sun was blessing us with its visible rays, offering us warmth, enveloping us, wrapping us up with sincerity.

It all looked new to me today.

* * *

Later in the afternoon, I stopped by my parents' house on my way to the supermarket to return a dish of leftovers my mother had given to me. I rang the door, but no one appeared to be home.

When I turned around, I saw Michael's dad out on the driveway collecting his mail. He look as if he'd just returned from a walk, and I waved to him, my confidence much higher than it had been in years past. He saw me approaching.

"Hello, Annabelle," he said cheerfully.

"Hi," I said. "How are you, Mr. Contelli?"

"Not too bad," he said. "Just wishing for warmer weather. Ready to head to Florida for vacation."

"When do you leave?" I asked him.

"Two weeks."

"Is Michael home?" I asked.

"No, he isn't. He left this morning for New York. He's getting his apartment in order because he starts his new job in two weeks. Lots to do, I guess."

"Oh, that's right," I said playing it off, but wishing it weren't happening. I had to think quickly. "Any chance you have his number? "

"He doesn't have one yet. He's staying at the Washington Square Hotel for a few days. I have the address of the apartment inside; he wrote it down for us. I can get it for you if you'd like. Come on in."

I followed him into the house where he had a fire going full blast; the warmth of it heated up the room. He jotted down the information on a small piece of note paper and handed it to me. I thanked him and began to leave.

"I'm glad you two patched things up," he said. "And I'm sorry for both Carol's and my behavior in it all."

I always loved his dad, so genuine and kind, just like his son. I had been the one at fault; they just reacted to my behavior.

"I'm sorry I did what I did. You'll never know how much," I said. It had become easier to say it out loud.

He nodded. There was nothing more to say.

I walked out the door, turned to him, and waved the paper in the air. "Thanks for this," I said with a smile, and disappeared.

* * *

On the morning of New Year's Eve, I drove out to St. Michael's to visit Vivi. It had become a tradition of ours to meet for brunch at the Town Dock Restaurant on the water. The drive helped me sort out my thoughts and future plans. I always enjoyed my ride to the Eastern Shore; Route 50 was a straight shot all the way to the exit for St. Michael's. The highway was flat, minus the four miles of the Bay Bridge you cross to get over the Chesapeake. It was quiet, and there were few cars on the road. It was partly cloudy; the sun would sneak out every now and then just to tease us with some warmth. I was looking forward to our get-together, primarily because I always enjoyed speaking with Vivi when my parents were not around. Although my mother had been less argumentative since her battle with cancer, it was easier to speak with Vivi alone, without my mother's constant scrutiny, though it had become more infrequent as time had passed. Sometimes I wondered where the depth of my mother's resentment used to come from, though I may have finally pieced it together. My mother strived to be fiercely independent, however, I don't think she ever succeeded. She relied on my father far too much. Vivi was able to be strong and live alone after my grandfather's passing. I wasn't sure my mother ever quite got over that loss. I was quite sure Vivi continued to miss him, but they handled it in different ways. I remembered one day my mother asked Vivi if she would marry again. Vivi responded, "I don't know if I ever could, Donna. It's hard to replace something that was nearly perfect."

My mother had become anxious about Vivi being alone, and I think my mother worried. But my grandmother proved that she could survive on her own and that she relished her life as it was, with an abundance of friends, social activities, and family nearby. It was something to be admired. In fact, I had used Vivi as an inspiration when I had enough of Cole and knew that being on my own was better than being in a debilitating relationship.

She was waiting for me at the hostess desk, smiling.

"That's a new coat!" I said, as I kissed her.

"I got it on sale at Charisma's on Monday when I got back. I'd been eyeing it in the window."

"It's very nice," I said to her, "I like this color. . .what do they call it?"

"Salmon."

"It becomes you," I said.

We were seated at a table by the window, and the waiter brought us two glasses of water with lemons. We each ordered Eggs Benedict and scones and mimosas to toast the New Year.

"So, are you going with Claudia to the clubhouse tonight?"

"Yes," she said. "I'm actually very excited. Fred and Ted are going to play, and all the old fogies are going to dance and get loaded on two drinks. Just like always."

"I can't believe that's the name they decided on, 'Fred and Ted.'"

"Well, those are their names! What would you have them call themselves, 'Fred and Ethel?'"

I laughed at her—she was in one of her funny moods. "They've been practicing since summer. I think they have about thirty songs under their belts. God only knows if any of them are good," she said.

Fred Thomas and Ted Abernathy were two gentlemen my grandmother had been friends with since she moved there. They were best friends with my grandfather, and Fred's wife, Claudia, was my grandmother's best friend. Ted's wife passed away two years ago. He had a beautiful, smooth, Perry Como-style voice and Fred could bang a piano like no senior I'd ever seen. They started playing together years ago and finally were talked into being this year's entertainment at the annual New Year's Eve party. Vivi seemed excited about it, and I was thrilled for her.

When the topic of Michael came up, I filled her in on Cole's visit and Michael's unexpected, but sweet gesture, to come over and then explained that he'd gone to New York to get settled as he prepared to start his new job. I was waiting to tell her what I was going to do.

The mimosas arrived, and Vivi held hers up and began to make a toast.

"I'm going to be seventy-one years old this year," she said, "though I still feel like I'm fifty-one, and I wish for you as happy a life as I've had."

"Here's to you, Vivi," I said.

"And to you," she said. "What's that smirk for?"

I could hardly contain my excitement.

"I think I am about to do something completely crazy and out of character for me, Vivi."

"What?"

"I have this insane notion that I'm going to drive to New York when I leave here and surprise Michael. I'm hoping that his gesture the other night meant something."

"You mean besides that he's the nicest guy we know?"

"Exactly. The fact that he could be in the same room with me on Christmas Eve and then want to check on me after my fight with Cole makes me believe that maybe, just maybe, there's something that lingers between us. And even though it scares the living daylights out of me that he may not think we have any hope, I think I'd kick myself even harder if I don't tell him how I feel. This is different than an 'I'm sorry.' This is about my love for him. He deserves to hear this, too, even if he may not feel the same way."

Vivi looked at me, and a wicked smile plastered her face.

"Well, Missy, thank God it didn't take you ten years to make this decision," she said.

* * *

On the drive up the New Jersey Turnpike, I was nervous, hoping my scheme would work. I hadn't felt the butterflies of nervous euphoria in years. After I saw him sleeping on my couch, I had come to the conclusion that I always wanted to see him sleeping on my couch. I wanted to see him in the morning and at night. I wanted to talk with him like we did the other evening; it came so easily. I wanted to grow old with him. I'd lived my life without him for too long, and if anything remained between us, and if he could move on from our past, I'd feel incomparable euphoria. On the flip side, if he no longer had feelings for me, at least I could say I gave it a shot. It wouldn't be easy to move on from it, but it would certainly hurt less than never trying.

My small overnight bag was in the back of the car, and I knew I was insane to attempt the drive into New York on New Year's Eve. I decided to park in a public lot in Hoboken and took the Path in where I could walk to his hotel. I had called earlier in the day and the receptionist told me he indeed had a room booked for the night. I told them to let him know that a package would be arriving for him at six-thirty and that he had to be present to sign for it. I waited on one extension while they called him on another to tell him the situation: the receptionist fibbed and told him it was a large freight package and that his signature was needed. I put her up to it and planned to give her a big tip when I arrived. He agreed to wait for the call from the desk.

Had I lost my mind tracking him down like that? Ever since I first saw him, I realized that I loved him, loved him still, always loved him. There was no question it was me who had to salvage it, if it was even salvageable at all.

I found my way to the garage that I'd mapped out, locked the car, picked up my overnight bag, and ran to the Path station along with hundreds of other frenzied people who were attempting to become part of the New Year's mayhem. I was hurrying. I didn't want to miss this opportunity. I couldn't afford to miss it again.

I emerged from the Path in the Village and looked around. The hotel was only two blocks away. Shivers ran up my spine.

We were old friends, the city and I. It only took a moment for me to reacquaint myself with it. It was an amalgamation of scents, sounds, and visuals—the architecture of the buildings, the racket of honking cabs, the rush of people walking the streets, the scent of roasted chestnuts, and the buzz of New Year's excitement.

Adrenaline pulsed through my pores. I was alive and carefree. I was unafraid and impulsive. I was poetry and drama. I was a risk-taker and a romantic.

Michael

It was New Year's Eve, and the front-desk receptionist buzzed me at six twenty-five and announced that I had a delivery. She had sent a bellhop up so I could sign the paperwork for it. I couldn't imagine what it was, though I suspected my mother was up to something, like when she had a leather recliner delivered to my flat in London when I received a promotion and moved to a larger flat. I couldn't move into my apartment for several days, so I hoped whatever she'd sent wasn't too big—I didn't have anywhere to store it.

The knock came minutes later, and I unlatched the door to answer it. What was standing before me was not at all what I expected, but was instead the most beautiful delivery I'd ever received.

"I love you too much to let you go away again without trying, Michael," she said, almost out of breath, "and I know it won't be easy for you to trust that I'll never hurt you again, but I promise you—I promise you—that if you give me another chance, I won't let you down. I would never let you down."

Despite my fears and concerns—and the rational, logical me wanting to hold on to reservations about it all—my heart had none. I had loved her then, and I loved her as she stood before me. I was getting choked up as I looked at her, out of breath and emotional in the hallway, her bag flung over her shoulder, her eyes wide, as she searched for an answer. The gesture alone gave me a sense of hope.

I nodded, and she threw her arms around me, kissing me, her hands running through my hair, my hands holding her face, kissing her back, years of loss wrapped up together. We were in sync with the intensity of the city, its vitality. She was here, and it felt like I was home.

Part Four

Vivi

I never liked to throw my age around any more than I liked to tell someone that I knew better than they did. As Jonathan Swift once said, "A man should never be ashamed to own that he has been in the wrong, which is but saying... that he is wiser today than yesterday."

I shared this quote with my granddaughter recently when I was visiting her, and she copied it down and stuck it to her refrigerator. I had no doubt she would look at it often and remember, and when I was no longer around, she would recite it to her children, so they knew: we all make mistakes.

When you love someone as dearly as I loved her, you worried. You worried she'd make the wrong choices and prayed she would make the right ones instead. When she made a poor choice, you hoped and prayed that eventually she'd find her way, even if it took better than ten years for it to happen.

I'd been around long enough to know when two people were compatible and had what it took to make a relationship last. My husband Ben's untimely illness and subsequent death nearly killed me, though I didn't let on too much to anyone. The secret grieving I did was held in the privacy of my own home or as I lay next to his gravesite weeping into the tall grasses. I'd probably never recovered from that loss, and I supposed I never would.

That was one of the reasons for my concern with Annabelle. I didn't believe she had ever recovered. And for her, it may have been far worse: she had to live with guilt over her own actions, and the knowledge that the man she loved was alive, even if he was across an ocean for a period of time. The loss I suffered was out of my control, though God knows I would have changed it if I could have.

When she was finally able to apologize to Michael years later—the man she loved but mistakenly left—she came back to the person she had been, little by little. First, the mistake she made was forgiven, and second, she was able to repair something she never really wanted to damage in the first place. Some people were lucky that way.

Or was it destiny? I pondered this question because during the ten years they were apart, neither one of them ever found what they were looking for because what they were looking for had already been found, even if it required a rest stop. People grew up; they learned about themselves, and they understood more of the world around them. Annabelle loved to say that her therapist had a big hand in her growth, and she very well may have, but what Annabelle really needed was to explore herself more fully, understand the things that made her tick and acknowledge those things that made her happy or unhappy. Her therapist was just the conduit by which she could do it.

As for Michael, ever since he was a little kid, he always had a heart of gold. I saw it in him then, and I saw it in him three years ago on Christmas Eve. He grew, too, and because he was away from Annabelle, he became a stronger person—strong enough to forgive her and himself and never look back.

I set up the Pack-N-Play that she bought to leave at my house. Annabelle had an even bigger tummy than she did with the first one, and we were all expecting that a little girl might be in the cards. In the meantime, Benjamin walked for the first time, and I heard he can almost say "Vivi."

They decided to leave Manhattan and relocate somewhere in the Annapolis vicinity to be nearer to their families. Annabelle was offered her former faculty position at the college, and Michael's first book of fiction was set to launch. It was a work he'd been writing for years, and a publisher had taken interest in it several months ago.

I looked around at my gardens and wished I had more energy to take care of them properly, but I tired a little more quickly in my old age than I used to. Don't get me wrong, I wasn't bound to a rocking chair or anything like that; it was just that the bones ached a little more and the eyes were a little heavier by the time I settled down in front of the television at night. I still played music, organized card games at the clubhouse, assisted with events in St. Michael's, and did my own laundry. I even had a date planned for Saturday night with Ted, if you called playing poker and tinkering at the piano at the clubhouse a date.

I walked around the patio examining the flowers, their scents. My hydrangea bush was about to bloom, and the roses were blooming, their reds and yellows painting my landscape. It was funny how you remembered stories people told you and how you would cling to those memories you held most dear. Now that they'd purchased their first home together, I decided what I wanted to give Annabelle and Michael for their housewarming gift. It was sitting right there in its colorful pot—a mimosa tree—catching some sun, growing a little bit each day, getting ready for fall planting, its leaves and pink blossoms new and fresh, a little reminder of both their love for each other, and that, if we wanted to, we could grow and flourish from our mistakes.

♥

THE END

213

Book Club & Reading Group Questions for Discussion

1.   When the story opens, we hear Annabelle's thoughts regarding her newfound freedom. Do you think she had ever allowed herself to feel that type of independence before?

2.   Michael talked about needing to go home. After ten years, what prompted him to leave London and go back to the States?

3.   Why do you think both main characters "ran away" from their problems? Did they learn anything about themselves because they chose to run away?

4.   Why do holidays play a big part in the novel? Try to recount the holidays that are included and what happened at each one.

5.   How does the backdrop of Annapolis—and even London and New York—help us relate to the plot and the characters? If you've been to any of these places, does that heighten your interest in the story?

6.   What significance do the supporting characters play in the lives of Annabelle and Michael? Discuss the roles of Andie, Will, Delia, Andrew, Cole, and Janie.

7.   In Part Three, there are big changes that take place in the lives of Michael and Annabelle. How do they change? Are they different from how they were in Parts

One & Two? Discuss.

8. In Part Two, Annabelle asks Vivi the following questions: "Can you be independent and be married? Can marriage and being your own person co-exist?" In present day where more than half of marriages fail, do you think marriage and independence can co-exist?

9. There is one theme that continues to be examined by the characters in the book, and that's the theme of being forgiven for a mistake you've made. When you've been hurt by someone, is it easy to forgive mistakes, both the small and the big ones?

10. This story takes place before cellular phones were around—and before they were used in the manner in which they are today. The characters relied on letters to communicate some of their intimate thoughts. How might cell phones have changed the nature of this story?

11. What is the significance of the mimosa tree? What does it symbolize in the book?

12. Why is Part Four told in a different voice? What would have been different had Michael or Annabelle told the final chapter?

Acknowledgements

Special thanks to the following people who helped this book come to fruition:

My critical readers and editors including Cheryl Klein, Chip Rouse, Leni Parrillo, Diana Mark, Jim Abbiati, and Anthony Verni;

My brave inaugural audience, who read first and second drafts including Amy Nelson, Currie Hinz, Michelle Kruhm, and Julie Wagner;

My current and former students and supportive colleagues at Stevenson University for allowing me to share with them the trials and tribulations of writing and self-publishing;

Retired Towson University professor, Dr. George Freidman, who told me to write this novel years ago, as well as National University's creative writing professors for pushing me;

Readers of Steph's Scribe and tolerant friends who have allowed me to discuss the book and the process;

The services of Nicola Ormerod for helping prepare the novel for digital publication;

My dear friend and photographer, Jennifer Bumgarner, for understanding the book and making the cover photo come to life;

My in-laws, Mark and Jo Verni, for their support and encouragement;

My children, Matthew and Eleanor, for understanding why mommy was locked up in her office trying to get this novel just the way she wanted it;

My parents, Leni and Doug Parrillo, for their constant support and love, and for raising me in Annapolis;

And finally, to my husband, Anthony—I couldn't have done it without you. Thank you for inspiring Michael and helping me find his voice. This is for you, with love.

♥

Dear Readers,

Letters play an important part in "Beneath the Mimosa Tree," so I thought I would write one to you, readers, to say thank you. I can't tell you what it means to me that you selected this piece of fiction. I know there are many quality novels out there for you to read and dissect, and that's why I'm so appreciative that you decided to take the time with this one.

It was an absolute pleasure writing and crafting Michael and Annabelle, and I hope you enjoyed getting to know them as much I enjoyed creating them and their story.

I hope we cross paths again sometime in the future.

With Gratitude,
Stephanie

About the Author

STEPHANIE VERNI was born in Fort Knox, Kentucky, and grew up in Maryland. Her teenage years and a portion of her adult years were spent living in Annapolis and Baltimore. A graduate of Towson University, she earned her first master's degree in Professional Writing from Towson University, and a second master's degree (MFA) in Creative Writing from National University. She spent thirteen years working in public relations and publishing for the Baltimore Orioles baseball club. For the past four years, she has been a full-time faculty member of Business Communication at Stevenson University outside of Baltimore where she serves as an associate professor. She teaches feature writing, magazine writing, public relations writing, and advertising. She resides in Severna Park, Maryland, with her husband and two children. For more information about Stephanie and her work, visit her author website at stephanieverni.com, or follow her blog, Steph's Scribe, at stephsscribe.com.